JUSTICE NEVER SLEEPS

A NOVEL OF MURDER AND REVENGE IN SPOKANE

Other Books of Interest from Marquette Books

John M. Burke, *From Prairie to Palace: The Lost Biography of Buffalo Bill* (2005).
ISBN: 0-922993-21-1

Tichenor, Phillip J., *Athena's Forum: A Historical Novel about a Swedish Owned Newspaper in 19th Century America* (2005).
ISBN: 0-922993-27-0

Tonya Holmes Shook, *The Drifters: A Christian Historical Novel about the Melungeon Shantyboat People* (2005).
ISBN: 0-922993-19-X

David Demers, *Dictionary of Mass Communication & Media Research: A Guide for Scholars, Students and Professionals* (2005).
ISBN: 0-922993-25-4

John C. Merrill, Ralph D. Berenger and Charles J. Merrill, *Media Musings: Interviews with Great Thinkers* (2004).
ISBN: 0-922993-15-7

Ralph D. Berenger (ed.), *Global Media Go to War: Role of Entertainment and News During the 2003 Iraq War* (2004).
ISBN: 0-922993-10-6

C. W. Burbank, *Beyond Zenke's Gate* (2004).
ISBN: 0-922993-14-9

David Demers, *China Girl: One Man's Adoption Story* (2004).
ISBN: 0-922993-08-4

Larry Whitesitt, *Northern Flight of Dreams: Flying Adventures in British Columbia, Yukon, NW Territories and Alaska* (2004).
ISBN: 0-922993-09-2

Melvin L. DeFleur and Margaret H. DeFleur, *Learning to Hate Americans: How U.S. Media Shape Negative Attitudes Among Teenagers in Twelve Countries* (2003).
ISBN: 0-922993-05-X

JUSTICE NEVER SLEEPS

A Novel of Murder and Revenge in Spokane

L. Ray Edwards

MB Marquette Books Spokane WA

Copyright © 2005 by Marquette Books

All rights reserved. No part of this publication may be reproduced, stored in a retrieval system, or transmitted in any form or by any means, electronic, mechanical, photocopying, microfilming, recording, or otherwise, without permission of the publisher.

This book is a work of fiction. Names, characters, places, and incidents either are products of the author's imagination or are used fictitiously. Any resemblance to actual events or locales or persons, living or dead, is entirely coincidental.

Printed in the United States of America

Library of Congress Cataloging-in-Publication Data

Edwards, L. Ray (Lonnie Ray), 1965-
  Justice never sleeps : a novel of murder and revenge in Spokane / L. Ray Edwards.
    p. cm.
  ISBN 0-922993-26-2 (pbk. : alk. paper)
  1. Spokane (Wash.)--Fiction. 2. Revenge--Fiction. I. Title.
  PS3605.D889J87 2005
  813'.6--dc22
                                    2005006133

MARQUETTE BOOKS
3107 E. 62nd Avenue
Spokane, WA 99223
509-443-7057
books@marquettebooks.org
www.MarquetteBooks.org

To

Lynn and Sean,
the culmination of my life's highest and best aspirations.
I love you both more than I know how to express.

Acknowledgments

I hesitated to include this page, because inevitably I will leave someone out who should have been here. I apologize in advance.

Here, in no particular order, are people who have my gratitude:

• Molinda Goforth, my mother, without whom this author would not have been possible;

• Kris Edwards, who is dear to me despite his love of Linux;

• Mark Edwards, who has made me proud over and over and who always kicked my butt at sports;

• John and Nellie Schwegler, for undying support, belief, and love;

• Pat Edwards and Lon Miracle, my two great fathers;

• Jay and Kevin and Bob, who saw me through good times and bad and who never fail to make me laugh and also taught me that "fog" is way funnier than "cloud," that dust can make one sleepy, and that sometimes you just "don't want to go," even if that's lame;

• Robin Helton, my good friend and "other brother," it is good that we met and we'll probably just stay on the train until it reaches the station, won't we?;

• Steve Cody, who has been a close friend, a trusted

adviser, and a profound influence on my life;

• Larry Wilson, a "magnificent son of a bitch"—those were very good days indeed;

• Scott Mahalick, for inspiration, support, and good advice;

• Bob Glasco, for reminding me of the story of the two bulls—may the old bull prevail, always!;

• Dan O'Day, who inspires and motivates in more ways than he probably realizes;

• Jim Sykes, a.k.a. "Li'l Pony"—Jimbo, that little bird was right;

• Tony and Kathy Trovato, for being the good friends that they are and for sharing Crazy Jack and Scary Santa with us.

• Kyle Clardy, the Pablo Picasso of ProTools, and my "other son";

• Bob O'Dell, who gave me a whole new vocabulary, "Here's the new plan";

• Dave Tester, a good friend and a Great Radio Guy;

• Jim Diamond, a kindred spirit who has the best set of vocal cords this side of the Rockies, who knows the meaning of Dees Sleaze, and why you might want to wrap tape around the capstan;

• And the Nanninga clan of Bob, Betty, Denise, Valerie (and Blaine, Ira, Megan and Melanie)—my life would have been a much poorer one without all of you in it.

This book is a work of fiction; I humbly acknowledge the source of true justice and redemption, the Lord Jesus Christ.

Ray Edwards
Summer 2005

Chapter 1

I was sitting in my doctor's office, watching a fly bang its head against the window. Dr. Bibbs, seeing that the fly was a great distraction for me, killed it with a newspaper.

"So are we to the gods," I said. Bibbs just stared at me.

It became apparent he wasn't going to catch up, so I helped him.

"It's Shakespeare," I said. "'As flies to wanton boys, are we to the gods; they kill us for their sport.'"

Black thoughts to be having while sitting in your doctor's office, I guess, but there it is.

"Mister Black," said Dr. Bibbs, licking his lips, "I'm not sure I understand your train of thought. Have you been listening to me?"

I smiled, noticing the congruence between my name and the blackness of my thoughts.

Dr. Bibbs seemed annoyed that I was drifting away from our conversation. His plump fingers were splayed out on the mahogany desktop, his wedding ring far too small for his ring finger. The ring was so tight it looked as if it were imbedded in the flesh of his finger. He will never get that ring off, I imagine.

"Mister Black?" he said. The volume was slightly louder this time.

"King Lear," I said, finishing my display of Shakespearean

trivia. "I'm sorry, Doc. You were saying something about the area of my brain that regulates sleep, I think. And call me Quinn, will you? I don't like 'Mister Black.'"

I have always hated being called "Mister Black"—it just doesn't sound very nice. I endured a period in my high school years when I was often called "The Reverend Mister Black," something which caused me to loathe the Kingston Trio from that time forward. Not that it really mattered at this particular moment, but "just call me Quinn" was a habit, and these days I survived mainly on habit.

Dr. Bibbs grimaced, the roll of fat under his neck pushing out against his starched white collar. His thin black little mustache folded under his nose to the point of becoming nearly invisible. The mustache was the only black hair on his head—his eyebrows and the hair on his head were stark white.

"Yes, of course—Quinn," he continued. I guess he was glad to have my attention again, but he sounded uncomfortable using my first name. He wanted to tell me about areas in my brain that control sleep function, and I wasn't making it easy for him. "The bullet apparently damaged the area of your brain that controls and regulates sleep, yes. That's the cause of your insomnia."

I laughed.

"Doc, I haven't slept a single hour since I came out of the coma. It seems like it ought to have a name more impressive than 'insomnia.'"

"Quinn, I don't think you're taking this seriously. You're very lucky to be alive. You're very lucky that you aren't paralyzed, or still in a coma."

"If I'm so lucky, why do you want me to be serious?" I asked.

"Because you were not so lucky to have this damage to your brain. It's hard for us to know what the inability to sleep will mean to your long-term health."

He leaned forward, as if trying to emphasize his point. I noticed that there was plenty of room on his desk for him to place his elbows. His desk was immaculate—there was a pen holder with two gold-plated ink pens, a desk calendar, and two wooden trays, one with a brass sign saying "In" and the other with a matching brass sign saying "Out." There was a phone on the desk, and a notepad with no notes on it. Very neat, very orderly.

"Mister Black," he said, "sleep is essential to your physical and psychological well-being. I'd like to do some further tests."

"What do you hope to learn?" I said.

He seemed surprised by this question. In fact, he leaned back in his leather chair, as if the surprise had struck him in the chest. His chair squeaked, like good leather does. He sighed.

"Honestly, I'm not sure. There are very few cases like this one on record, and none with good documentation."

I looked out the window behind him, and I could see the emergency room parking lot down on the first floor. Actually, I didn't remember being brought in through those big double doors, but I suppose I had been. It seemed like a lot longer than six weeks ago.

I felt the stubble on my head where my hair was growing back, and ran my finger along the scars on the back of my skull. Hard to believe that Doctor Bibbs's fingers had been inside there—inside my head, cutting out pieces of my brain to get at the bullet and to reduce the swelling. Hard to believe I was sitting here now in Dr. Bibbs's very pretentious and orderly office, discussing my inability to sleep. I was thirty-five years old; I had a very rare brain disorder that prevented me from sleeping; my wife was dead; my doctor seemed to think me a very interesting medical anomaly. What was the point of all this?

"I don't want any more tests," I said. "I've had enough."

Bibbs shook his head.

"Quinn," he said, fingering a button on his Nautica shirt, "I have no idea how your body is going to respond to a total lack of REM sleep. At least not over the long run. Most experts in the field agree that a certain amount of REM is necessary each night for healthy mental function. You could start experiencing severe psychological dysfunction after a while—and then there are possibly serious physical problems as well."

I heard him, but I was thinking about Angie again. If she were in the room with me now, I thought, we would have looked at one another and smiled. In that smile, we would have known how funny we found Dr. Bibbs—no words would have passed between us, but we would have known.

I could see her smile so clearly. *He hasn't got a clue*, her smile would say.

As for Doctor Bibbs, there was very little chance that he would ever have a clue. He had no idea what mattered to me right now.

Didn't he know my wife was dead?

Did he think anything else in this world was more important? The fact that at thirty-five years of age, my life was now stripped of all direction and meaning.

I already knew about my medical condition, of course. I knew this whole rap about what happens when you don't sleep—I probably knew it better than Dr. Bibbs. I had spent the last few weeks thinking and reading about little else. After all, I was on leave from my work at the radio stations and had nothing but time on my hands. I had to do something during those eight hours every night when most people were sleeping.

I said, "Actually, there is some documentation. There was a case in 1972, a Viet Nam combat soldier named Frank Carter, struck in the head by shrapnel. Didn't sleep for almost a year."

Bibbs looked at me, and breathed deep, almost like a sigh.

"The shrapnel penetrated his brain in the same basic area

that the bullet penetrated mine," I said. It was interesting to note the absence of emotion in my voice. "Within three months he started falling apart mentally. Inside of a year he was dead."

Dr. Bibbs was staring at me now, like I was a very strange bug.

"Oh, I've done my homework, Doc. I've got a library card. I've got the Internet. I've got nothing but time on my hands. I've had a lot of sleepless hours to read up on this. I know that nobody has ever had this kind of injury and lived very long."

He grunted and then continued.

"No one has had this exact injury, Quinn. Your case could be different."

He had stopped fiddling with the button on his shirt. I think he was really paying attention to me for the first moment since I had walked into his office. Score one for the bug.

"I've read the background material, Dr. Bibbs." I recited, "'Patients unable to attain REM sleep—Rapid Eye Movement, commonly known as dreaming—suffer serious psychological and physiological effects. Dementia, delirium, fever, heart attack, stroke, grand mal seizures. In all cases the condition eventually leads to a mental breakdown and then to death.'" I looked at Dr. Bibbs. "Am I right?"

For the first time this morning, he met my eyes.

"Yes."

"So your tests would tell you what, exactly?"

He shifted his weight in his seat. The leather creaked.

"They might prove useful in the study of this kind of injury in future patients."

"I'm more interested in something that would be useful now, to this patient," I said.

"There's always that possibility, Quinn," he said. He sounded sympathetic. I suppose he really was. I decided to stop being so hard on him. What was the point? He wasn't the guy who had put the bullet in my head.

For the thousandth time, I wondered about the man who had shot me. Why? Who had I ever harmed? Who had Angie ever harmed?

Bibbs was staring at me again, and I felt as though I had to cut him a little slack.

"Okay then, Doc. You can have your tests. But only on an outpatient basis. I'm done staying in the hospital."

He leaned forward again.

"But, Quinn—"

I stood up.

"No 'buts,' Doc. I've been in the hospital too much since Angie's death. I may not have long to live myself, and I intend to do the living I have left outside the hospital, not in it. Anyway, somebody's gotta feed my dog."

I turned for the door, and he scrambled to get up. Thinking of my dog made me decide to throw the doctor one more bone.

"Set up the tests, and let me know when they are. You can leave me a message. I have a machine. I'll try to make it in."

I opened the door, and he waddled up behind me. Had to waddle, because he was so fat. There's something wrong with having a fat doctor, I thought.

"Quinn, I'm not sure you know what's important here."

"Physician, heal thyself," I said.

Chapter 2

On that perfect day, the last one, the one I wish I could suspend in time, we were buying a dog.

I had never really liked dogs, a trait I probably inherited from my father—or maybe I didn't inherit it but rather acquired it through imitation. Either way, getting a dog had never been a high priority for me. At least not until Angie decided she wanted one. Then it became important not only that I get a dog, but also important that I get a very specific *kind* of dog.

"They're called West Highland Terriers," Angie said. She was pointing to a picture in a large book. The book was on her knees. I was looking at the knees and not at the book—a fact which she noticed.

"Quinn!"

She punched me in the shoulder and I pretended to wince. She liked to think she was strong.

She smiled. That always seemed to unravel me, and I suspect she knew it.

"Quinn, would you look at the dog, please?"

Her hair was so blond that the only thing better than its color was the knowledge that it didn't originate from a bottle. She brushed it back away from her eyes and smiled at me again. I looked at the picture of the dog.

Apparently these West Highland Terriers were small dogs,

white with stubby legs and faces that made them look like petulant little old men. Little old men with grudges and politics.

"Couldn't we get something—" I looked for the right word, but all I could come up with was, "bigger?"

Angie wrinkled up her nose and shook her head.

I remember that on this particular day she was wearing a white knit top and red cotton shorts, and a silly plastic necklace that Stacy had made for her. Angie always wore these little gifts that her niece made, just as she always hung up the dreadful pictures that Stacy painted. I had argued on more than one occasion that she could have just said "thank you"—and never worn the plastic jewelry or displayed the finger-paintings—but Angie felt that this would have been fundamentally dishonest.

She wore the jewelry with pride.

She displayed the art prominently and enjoyed looking at it.

These are some of the reasons I loved her. Those were good days—mere weeks in the past but now seemingly part of another lifetime. Those were the days by which I would measure the rest of my life, although I was not wise enough to know it then.

Back then, I could only think about the future. About how we would someday be happy if only we met a long list of conditions: *if only* I got promoted, *if only* Angie finished law school and got on with a good firm, *if only* we could pay off our student loans, *if only* we could get a new car. At that time we had a long list of "if onlies," and no idea that none of them mattered.

In those days all I could think about was the future, and now all I can think about is the past.

How was I supposed to appreciate the incredible good fortune of sitting next to my beautiful young wife, my skin touching hers, arguing with her about the kind of dog we were going to get?

How was I to have an appreciation for the value of those moments? Of the gentle curve her neck made just behind her ear, or the mischievous way she licked her lips after smiling and glancing at me sideways.

"And what kind of dog do you want?" she asked.

I thought about this for a moment. I knew I had to be careful.

"Hmmm. A German Shepherd?"

She shifted a little closer to me and slid her arm around my back, shaking her head "no." I remember she smelled like peaches.

"Siberian Husky?" I offered. I was getting a little light-headed, because she was dragging her long fingernails up and down my back.

She shook her head again, and placed her other hand on my knee. The book slid to the floor.

She licked her lips.

"West Highland Terrier?" I asked. I think my voice came out as more of a whisper.

She smiled and said, "Yes."

She kissed me, pressing in against me and pushing me back on the couch. I remember wondering if I was going to have a heart attack.

We went to pick up our "Westie," as Angie referred to it, that afternoon.

It was a Saturday in May, and the breeder's place was just outside of Spokane, sitting all alone in the middle of an expansive sea of wheat fields, looking a little small and lonely. The driveway was at least a quarter of a mile long, and each side was littered with old farm implements, which I thought were junk, but which Angie informed me were art.

"It's rustic," she said, as if I should be able to puzzle it out from there.

The driveway ended in a loop, with the house at one side of the circle and a barn-like structure—which I assumed was the kennel—at the other side. There were two parking spaces in front of the kennel, and we parked in one of them. There was a tricycle in the other one.

As we got out of the car, I could hear the sound of dogs barking inside the kennel, the noise echoing inside the metal building.

The front door opened into a tiny room with a counter, two chairs, and a coffeepot sitting on a corner table. The coffee smelled like hot asphalt, as if it had been made hours ago and then just sat there cooking on the hot plate. Behind the Formica counter, a man of indeterminate age sat reading a copy of *Soldier of Fortune*, and he looked up as we came in, his mouth hanging open.

I whispered to Angie, "Even the people are rustic."

She jabbed me in the ribs with her elbow, and she smiled at the man with all her teeth. They were white and straight, and quite possibly some of her more dangerous weapons.

The man, who was pasty and balding with thick pink lips, closed his mouth for a moment but showed no other sign of life. I suppose he was all tuckered out from his latest adventure as a soldier of fortune.

"I'm here about the Westie pup," Angie said as she approached the counter. I let the door close behind me; it was on a spring and the tension was set too high, so it slammed loudly. The man behind the counter licked his pasty lips, making them into slimy lips, and smiled. His dental work was not as impeccable as Angie's.

"My name's Kelso," he said. "Me and my brother own the place."

As if on cue, another man appeared from a door just behind the counter, and as it opened the sound of the barking dogs became a crescendo. He closed the door, wiping his hands on a rag and smiling.

"You must be the Blacks," he said. I nodded. He stepped around the counter and put out his hand.

"I'm Nate. Kelso's my brother. I've got your dog around back—just lettin' him take care of business so's he doesn't do it in you car on the way home."

I shook Nate's hand, and watched Kelso, who still had not moved from his chair. Kelso glared at me and went back to his magazine. Where Kelso was slightly fat and pale, his brother Nate was lean and tan.

We followed Nate outside, and once the door closed he said, "You have to excuse Kelso. He's a little slow. I don't usually have him minding the desk, you know, dealing with people and all, but one of our bitches is sick and I was tending to her."

"It's okay," Angie said sweetly. "He seems very nice."

Nate looked at her for a moment, as if he were waiting for her to say something else, and then he proceeded to walk around the side of the building. We followed. The pup was there, in an outdoor dog run made of chain link fencing. He was rolling around on his back, a mass of white fur with a bright pink tongue hanging from one end. He was small and fluffy.

"Powderpuff!" Angie said, and she ran to the gate clapping her hands together. "His name is Powderpuff."

Silently, I vowed to begin a campaign of shortening his name to "Powder," but when Angie glanced at me for approval I merely smiled. One had to play these things just right.

She was already opening the gate and scooping the terrified little dog up into her arms, and I was discussing payment with Nate. As I watched Angie playing with her new puppy, I felt for an instant that timeless sense that all is right in the world.

I might have paid more attention had I known this would be the last time I would feel truly happy.

Chapter 3

We didn't get much sleep that night.

We tried putting the puppy in a box in the kitchen, but that didn't work. He just cried and howled until we finally caved in and came to his rescue. We stumbled down the hallway to the kitchen, and I looked at the clock on the microwave—2:30 a.m. The puppy's tail beat the side of the box. His tongue was hanging out. He looked as if he were smiling. He knew he had won. Angie scooped him up out of the box and held him up under her chin, with her lip poking out like a little girl about to cry.

"All right," I sighed. "He can sleep with us."

We shuffled back to the bedroom together. I didn't even think twice about the back door being unlatched.

Now I think about it a lot.

I was awakened by a loud noise—though in that strange world of sleep, I could not have named what the noise was. Now of course, I know. But then, in that moment, I couldn't put it together. In fact, as I rolled over and looked at the glowing numbers on the alarm clock, I wasn't even really sure if I had heard a noise at all. I looked at the clock—4:07 a.m.

"Hey, did you hear something?" I whispered to Angie.

Angie didn't answer.

She wasn't there. Powderpuff was lying on Angie's pillow, looking at me as if he were wondering what I would do next, his head cocked to one side.

I heard a loud bang from the kitchen, like the door slamming. I remember thinking that Angie must have gotten one of her late-night cravings for Nilla wafers, and that she was most likely slamming the cupboard doors in search of a box of them.

As I stepped into the kitchen, it took a moment for me to figure out what I was looking at. As I started piecing the scene together, I could feel the cold hand of terror slip its fingers around my neck. My stomach tightened. I could hear the sound of my own breathing.

Angie was lying on the floor, her nightgown ripped down the back and her nude body exposed. Her left leg was turned at an odd angle, and her mouth and eyes were open. The expression on her face was one of surprise, but her eyes had a curious glassy look, as if she were looking at something miles in the distance. A trickle of blood ran from her mouth.

A stream of blood crept slowly away from her lips.

My mind seized. I couldn't accept what I was seeing.

I heard a noise from the living room, and turned to see a man standing behind me. I will never forget his face. Bony, high cheeks, skin pock marked by acne, thin arching eyebrows, hair cropped close to his head as if he were in the military.

He smiled.

To this day I am haunted by that smile. It told me he knew what he had done, that he had in fact been watching me and somehow he had enjoyed seeing my reaction to his brutality. One of his front teeth protruded slightly in front of the other.

I remember seeing a rivulet of perspiration run down the crevice of a scar on the left side of his face.

I will never forget that face.

He raised his right hand. There was a pistol in it—a .38-

caliber, nickel-plated, world-famous Saturday Night Special.

A spray of something red fanned out across the front of the man's white shirt, and I wondered what it was. I remember seeing the man lower the gun, and then another shower of blood pulsed from the side of my head, and I knew I had been shot.

That's the last thing I remember from my former life.

Chapter 4

Stan Ramsey was sitting at his desk at the Spokane Police Department when I entered the room. I had driven to the Police Headquarters straight from Dr. Bibbs's office and taken the steps at the front of the building two at a time, a newspaper tucked under my arm, almost like a man without a care in the world.

It took me a few minutes to get through the metal detectors at the front door, because the metal pins holding my skull together kept setting off the alarm. The guy running the security checks didn't believe me, and I finally had to flag down one of the citizen volunteers who knew me. She told the guy this happened every time I came in, and that she knew me, and that he should stop being a schmuck and let me through.

I found Ramsey finishing his lunch—a tuna sandwich and some Doritos. He was eating at his desk, his food resting on top of the plastic wrap for his sandwich. Underneath, his desk was covered with papers, files, unopened mail, and other assorted junk. I noted there were no gold-plated ink pens or wooden trays on his desk. He and Dr. Bibbs apparently held opposing views on what makes an efficient workspace.

He looked up as I approached his desk and smiled. I made a mental note that smiling while eating a tuna sandwich is not a good idea.

"Quinn, how are you?"

He put his sandwich down and shook my hand. His voice held that peculiar tone I heard from so many people these days, filled with shallow pity and sympathy. He doesn't have any idea what I've been through.

"I'm fine," I said, sitting down before he could offer me a chair.

He stood there looking at me for a moment before he went around to his side of the desk. I had thrown off his rhythm, I guess. But the fact is I was just tired and wanted to sit down—apparently not being able to sleep doesn't have any relationship to being tired.

"You look like shit," he said.

I nodded.

"You know why I'm here."

I tossed the *Spokesman Daily News* on his desk.

"Murder Suspect Freed," the headline said.

Ramsey didn't say anything. He just picked up a Dorito and chewed on it. He stared at the headline for a while. Finally, he said, "I guess I expected to see you today."

"Well?"

"Well, what? It's all right there in black and white," he said, pointing a Dorito at the newspaper.

"How is this possible?" I said.

Ramsey shifted in his seat.

"You've read the story, I assume, Quinn. I don't like it any better than you do."

I clenched my teeth, then forced my jaw to relax.

"The ruling came down yesterday. And nobody called me?"

He stared at me, chewing. I hated him at that moment.

"I still don't understand," I said. "We all know the guy did it. I was an eyewitness, for God's sake. So your guys screwed up the arrest. We still *have* the evidence. How can the court just disregard it?"

Ramsey shook his head.

"No, Quinn, we don't still have the evidence. All the real evidence we have came from what we found after the arrest. The gun, the clothing, everything. So when that all gets thrown out, we have only your testimony."

"Which is not enough?"

I hadn't really expected to hear anything new from him, but it was necessary for me to come here, to have him confirm the truth I already knew. After all the maneuvering, all the lawyers, all the depositions—it was over.

A fly landed on one of Ramsey's Doritos, but he didn't notice. I could have told him, or shooed the fly away I guess, but Stan Ramsey didn't mean all that much to me. To me he was just a cop who couldn't put away the beast that killed my wife. It seemed only natural that he should eat a certain amount of fly dung.

I stood up, as if I had somewhere to go. I stood there for a moment, and realized I *didn't* have anywhere to go. I sat back down.

"I can remember his face so perfectly," I said. "I can remember Angie on the floor. I can remember the blood trickling from her mouth. I can remember the sweat running down the side of that man's face. Why isn't that enough?"

"Quinn, stop this. You know why."

Yes, I knew. I didn't actually witness Danny Minor killing my wife. I hadn't seen him shoot me. All I had been able to remember during the hearing was the man's face, and the blood, and Angie on the floor, and the gun in his hand. I looked at Ramsey again, and saw no sympathy in his eyes this time. But I wasn't quite sure I even cared.

"You know as well as I do, Ramsey, that all that business about Minor hearing the shots and running into the house is nonsense."

Ramsey turned his hands palm-up and shrugged.

"It leaves us with nothing," Ramsey said. "All you have is circumstantial evidence. That's not enough for a prosecutor."

I stood up and walked away.

He didn't try to stop me.

I drove home.

Powder greeted me at the door, jumping and whirling in circles, barking in short bursts. His tail was wagging furiously. Angie would have been delighted, but at that moment I felt like crying. I attached the bright pink leash Angie had bought to his collar, and we left the house for our daily walk. For the first block or two, Powder urinated on every mailbox post we passed; finally he gave up, perhaps realizing he was out of ammo.

Angie was buried in the Saylor Memorial Gardens, next to her mother. Her grave was on the side of a little hill that overlooked the rest of the graveyard. There was a small marble bench nearby, and I usually sat there when I came to visit. I had sat on that bench with Powder every single day since I got out of the hospital.

Today there were no other visitors at the cemetery, except for one old man who I saw at the entrance as I drove in. He had been sitting on a tombstone, gesturing and talking at the sky with a big smile on his face. Most people would have thought he was nuts. Now I understood.

It was one of those glorious spring afternoons when the breeze is constant but gentle, and the sky was filled with big puffy white clouds set against a brilliant blue backdrop.

"The blues are blue and the greens are green," I said out loud. It was something Angie used to say. Powder cocked his head.

I could hear birds in the nearby trees, and someone else's dog barking somewhere in the distance. It was a perfect day, with the exception that my wife was dead and her killer was walking the streets of Spokane.

I looked at the words carved into the headstone: "Angela Renee Black—Beloved wife of Quinn Asher Black, 1968-2000."

It seemed a woefully inadequate statement about Angie's life. I should have come up with something more to put on the stone. Maybe one day I would figure out what that might be, and I could have a new stone made.

What was I to do now?

What was left?

I couldn't call on God. He seemed to have withdrawn from me completely, if He had ever really even been there. I hadn't thought seriously about God since my childhood, when I was forced to go to Sunday school.

Even if I could call on God, He wasn't going to bring Angie back.

According to the good doctor, I might well be dead myself within a few months, or even weeks. Certainly my life would never be the same. Danny Minor had seen to that. In one moment, he had taken all the meaning out of my life. The only thing left to me now was the hope that there might be some justice.

But even this had been denied. There would be no justice, not from the courts or from the law. Ramsey had made that clear.

A spider crawled across the front of the headstone on Angie's grave. A few weeks ago, I might have crushed it. Now I couldn't bring myself to do that. I watched it scurry along and then stop, lifting one of its front legs tentatively, then set the leg back down, then scurry some more. After a few minutes, it disappeared around the other side of the stone and was gone.

It occurred to me that if Danny Minor were here right now, I would have had no moral problem crushing him. The spider had worth; Danny Minor had none. I would have felt more guilt from killing the spider than I would killing Danny Minor.

I walked back down the hill. Powder trotted at my heals with his tongue lolling from one side of his mouth.

I knew what I had to do.

I might be a man who had very few days left to live, but I knew of at least one man who had fewer.

CHAPTER 5

I drove my car into the parking lot of Baxter's Pawn & Loan, which was too small and too close to the street. It was on Division, Spokane's major north-south thoroughfare—a strip commercial route, home to everything from Chinese buffet restaurants to used car lots.

Powder sat on the passenger seat beside me. I turned to him and said, "Wait here. I'll be back in a few minutes."

He barked once.

"Please don't pee in my car," I said. He stared at me and wagged his tail.

I got out of the car, pocketed the keys, and went inside.

There must be a rule that says all pawnshops are required to be dark and dingy—because every one I have ever been is like that. Baxter's was no exception. A man sat motionless behind the counter, wearing a cheap hairpiece, smoking a cheap cigar, and watching the U.S. Open on a cheap television. Why he was using that particular television when he had a wall full of better televisions across the room?

I approached the counter, and he turned toward me. It was eerie—his body didn't move. I suppose years of practice sitting in one place had made him very good at it. He gave the uncanny impression of being part owl.

"You need some help?" he asked, apparently slightly

irritated that I had interrupted his show.

"I need a pistol," I said.

"Yeah?" He rolled the stinky cigar from one side of his mouth to the other, using his tongue. It was not an appealing sight. "What for?"

"Revenge," I said, smiling.

He didn't smile back.

"I'll need a different answer before I can sell you a gun."

He pointed to the glass counter between us.

"There's what we got."

The case held more than two dozen pistols of different sizes and shapes, all lying on green velvet. I wondered about the green velvet, and it occurred to me that it looked a little worn. Perhaps it had come from a pool table.

I looked up at the sales clerk. He was watching me carefully while chewing his cigar.

"You Baxter?" I asked.

He laughed, which started up a series of phlegmmy coughs. He shook his head and said, "No, Bax is on the golf course, just like every day around this time. My name's Toomey."

I nodded.

"Look, I'm not sure exactly what I want," I said.

"No kidding."

I ignored the sarcasm and shook my head.

"I have some experience with weapons," I said. "But that was some time ago—and for a different purpose."

"What branch?"

I looked up at him.

"Marines."

He nodded.

"So what purpose was it you said you needed this particular weapon for?"

"Self-defense."

He looked skeptical.

Toomey grabbed a key from his belt without looking. It was on one of those big key rings where each key was attached to the master ring by a recoiling wire. Toomey opened the gun case and let the key zing back to his belt.

He reached inside the case and picked up one of the guns, a black Glock. He held it out and I took it. I was careful not to point it at either him or me. It seemed heavier than I thought it would. I had trained with firearms when I was in the Marine Corps Reserve, but it had been long time since I'd held a weapon, and I'm pretty sure Toomey knew it.

"That's a nine millimeter," he said. "Not too much recoil, which is good for tight spots. Nineteen rounds in the clip. It's light, and it's accurate. You can change clips in a few seconds."

I fumbled around and managed to get the clip out, and then slid it back in. It did not go as smoothly as one might have hoped. I was glad I hadn't elaborated on my weapons experience.

"How much?" I asked.

"Four hundred. Spare clip and shells are extra."

I paid for the gun, and Toomey told me I'd have to wait a few days for the background check before I could pick it up. The experience reminded me of an episode of *The Simpsons*, in which Homer wanted to buy a gun and was told he would have to wait for the background check. "But I'm mad now!" Homer had said.

I had laughed at that joke at the time. Now it didn't seem so funny.

I took my receipt and drove south on Division, defying my tradition of impatiently weaving in and out of the slow-moving traffic. Today I was content to ride in the far right lane, keeping a few car-lengths between me and the car in front of me. I had the windows down and the air conditioning on, and it occurred to me that Angie used to hate it when I did that. I turned off the air conditioning.

At that moment a strange feeling came over me. Everything seemed empty—like a shell, with no meaning or substance. I felt disconnected from reality, as if I were watching myself drive the car, as though I was observer.

This feeling lingered as I drove up South Hill and pulled into a space at Overlook Park. I got out of the car, sat on the hood, and looked down at the city below. The world felt hollow. I felt that if I had blown out my breath hard enough, the world would have just dissipated like smoke.

"Quinn, are you okay?"

The sound of the man's voice scared me enough that I literally leapt from the hood of my car and spun around to face him. My heart was pounding in my chest. It took me a few more seconds to realize the man was Ramsey.

"Ramsey," I said. It came out as a whisper.

He stepped around the front of the car and put a hand on my shoulder.

"Quinn, I said are you okay?"

I nodded, and brushed his hand from my shoulder.

"Yeah," I said. "Fine."

He was watching me with slitted eyes. That feeling of unreality was gone now. I had to pull myself together. What had happened to me? I looked in the front seat of the Blazer and saw Powder curled up and sound asleep. I glanced back at Ramsey.

"Well," he said, "you sure didn't look OK for a while. Do you know how long you've been sitting there, staring out into space?"

I shook my head.

"About forty minutes," he said.

Forty minutes. It had felt like no more than five.

What had happened to me?

"Well, I was thinking," I said, "in case you haven't noticed, Ramsey, I have a lot to think about."

He nodded, and popped a piece of gum in his mouth. He looked out at the city.

"Yeah," he said. "Like what you're planning to do with that piece you bought."

I looked at him, but he didn't look back at me. He just stared out at the city, making smacking noises with his gum.

"You were following me?"

"Sure. It's what I do. I'm a detective. I detect. And when you came into my office I detected something in your demeanor that I didn't like. So I followed you."

"To the cemetery? And then to Baxter's?"

"Yup."

I was quiet for a moment, not quite knowing what to say.

He kicked at the gravel under his feet and then finally looked me in the eye. "You bought that gun for self-defense, right?"

"Yeah, that's right."

"So you know that it's already too late to use it to defend Angela. Right?"

I looked at the ground.

"Angie."

He nodded.

"Sorry," he said. "Chances are they won't approve it anyway."

"The gun?" I asked.

He nodded. I was very disappointed that I hadn't thought of that on my own. Who would sell a gun to someone whose spouse had just been murdered a little three months ago? Then again, maybe their system of cross-checks wasn't that sophisticated.

I walked around the car and opened my door.

"I know what you're telling me, Ramsey. You're telling me not to be a vigilante."

He nodded. "And I'm telling you to be careful."

I didn't quite know what to make of that, so I said nothing. We looked at the lights of the city.

"Beautiful, isn't it?" Ramsey said.

"Haunt of jackals," I said.

"What?" He was looking at me as if I were speaking a foreign language.

"It's from the Bible," I said. "Jeremiah."

He stared at me.

"God is saying he will punish the people of Jerusalem for their wickedness—'I will make Jerusalem a heap of ruins, a haunt of jackals.' That's how it looks to me, Ramsey," I said, gesturing at the city below, "A haunt of jackals."

He pretended I hadn't said it.

"You sure you're OK?" he asked. "You really looked zoned out there for a while."

"Yeah, I'm fine."

I got in the car, closed the door, and started the engine.

When I pulled out onto the road, Ramsey was still standing there watching me.

Chapter 6

Charlie Ping and I had been friends since the Gulf War, where we served together in the Eight Engineering Battalion of the United States Marine Corps.

Charlie had been a full-timer. I was a reservist. The full-timers had a term for reservists—tampons. Because we were only useful once a month.

Ping's grandparents had been rounded up back in the forties and put into a concentration camp, at the height of the Japanese scare— never mind that the family was from China. Ping says his father was only three at the time, but had always sworn he could remember the days in the camp. He said his father had also sworn he wasn't bitter about it, and that neither were his grandparents. I've never been quite sure if I believed him. I would have been bitter.

Charlie and I became friends through necessity— we caught some fire out there in the desert, and we were pinned behind a tank with eight other men for seventeen hours, waiting for help to arrive, or waiting to die. We were pounded by artillery shells; in a short period of time, the tank was a smoking hulk of twisted metal, and only two of us were still alive. Ping was caught in the back of the head by a piece of shrapnel and rendered unconscious. I had carried him to safety on my back. We both received the Purple Heart, we were both lauded as heroes. These things made me feel as though I had perpetrated some kind of fraud. I'm convinced that most people would do the same things we had done. It just so happened that Ping and I had been lucky enough to survive.

I had gone to visit Ping at the hospital before we shipped home. Neither of us said much during the visit. I sat by his bed and we talked about what we would do when we got back home.

As I was leaving, Ping had said, "Quinn."

I had stopped at the foot of his bed.

"Yeah?"

"I owe you my life."

I shook my head. "No. What was I going to do, leave you there?"

Ping said, "A lot of men would have."

I shrugged.

He looked at me without glancing away as people normally do. That kind of eye contact is uncomfortable for most people. Finally, I said, "Maybe I'll call in the marker some day."

Ping nodded, and I left.

When we returned from the Gulf, we were both nearing the end of our tours, and we both opted out of the Corps. I went to back to my work in the advertising business, selling commercials for a company that owned several radio stations in Spokane; Ping bought a place just south of town on the Moran Prairie—about twenty acres, with a modest three-bedroom house in the center of the property.

"Good value," he had said at the time.

We had kept in touch over the years, visiting once or twice a year. We never talked about the Gulf.

I drove the car in front of Ping's house and killed the ignition. I had my windows rolled down, and a thin cloud of dust crept into the car.

The house was surrounded on all sides by woods, thick

stands of Douglas Firs and Aspens. The drive was a simple dirt road that most people probably never even saw as they drove past it, which was just the way Ping wanted it. He never seemed to be short of money, but he didn't appear to have a job. I had heard some rumors that he worked as a mercenary in overseas conflicts. I also heard that he collected debts from people who were in arrears with loan sharks. I never asked him about his work, though. It's just not something you'd ask Ping.

There were no signs of life around the house. No lights. Wrong. To my left was a black Great Dane, staring straight into my eyes. It had crept up on me and was looking at me through the open driver's side window, eye-level, her enormous mouth only inches from my face. I could feel her warm breath on my face.

I reached out my hand, and she licked the back of it.

"Hi, Brandy," I said. She backed up as I got out of the car.

"She's a fine girl," Ping said. He was standing behind the car, and I noticed he was cradling a rifle in his arms. Ping grinned and I grinned back.

Ping walked around the car and slapped me on the back. He was wearing khaki trousers and a crisp white tee-shirt. His hair was regulation short. Once a Marine, always a Marine.

"You look like hell," he said as we walked to the front porch.

"Ah, good," I said.

He stopped on the upper step to the porch and turned back to look at me.

"Good?"

I nodded.

"Yeah, 'cause I feel about three times worse. So at least I still got my looks."

Ping shook his head, and opened the front door.

"If you're counting on your looks to get you through," he said as I followed him inside, "you are in a world of hurt."

He was right.

I sat on the porch in an Adirondack chair, and Ping came out with two Scotches in paper cups. He set the bottle down between us.

He sat in the other chair and sipped his drink for a while. Brandy came bounding out of the woods and settled at his feet, looking up at him longingly as if the only thing required to complete her happiness would be for Ping to reach down and pet her. I reflected that Powder would likely fit in Brandy's mouth, legs and all, and was glad I had decided to leave him home. I penned him in the kitchen. I figured if he couldn't hold his excretions until I got back, they would be easier to clean off the linoleum than off the carpets in the rest of the house.

Ping set his drink on the small table between us and leaned over to scratch behind Brandy's ears, and she closed her eyes. Her happiness was, for the moment, complete. I could have told her that such things are fleeting.

"So you've made some kind of decision," Ping said at last.

I sipped my drink. "Yep."

He nodded.

"You've decided that the justice system has not worked its magic."

He concentrated on his work scratching Brandy's neck. She sighed. I looked out at the woods, noticing that it was hard to see the details now that the wood was in shadow. Although I couldn't see the horizon, I knew the sun was setting by the reddish glow in the sky.

"I need justice for her, Ping," I said. I didn't look at him. "I'm here to ask for your help. To ask if you really meant what you said about owing me a debt."

"I know," he said. He said nothing more. He was waiting for me to finish.

"I want to kill him, and I want you to help me," I said.

My voice came out in a whisper, coarse like a horse blanket, and my heart was beating hard. I drained my drink and set the cup on the table next to Ping's. After a moment's hesitation, I picked up his cup and drained that too.

Finally, Ping said, "Well, that settles it then. You can't drink and drive, so I guess you're staying here tonight."

He got up and went inside the house.

Of course, I did not sleep. I knew that I wouldn't sleep, but played along as if I were planning on going to bed. I simply didn't want to have to explain it to Ping.

He showed me my room, and I noticed that the furnishings in here were spare, just as in the rest of the house. There was a bed made up with crisp white sheets and a blanket. There was a night stand with an alarm clock—it was the wind-up kind, it was ticking, and it was set to the proper time. Since he hadn't known I was coming, I gathered that Ping kept it this way all the time. He always was one squared-away Marine.

After he had shown me the room and thrown an extra blanket at me, Ping said goodnight and closed my door. I listened as he made the rounds, and I knew he was checking the windows and doors to be sure they were closed and locked. Eventually the house grew quiet. I lay staring at the ceiling, listening to Ping's loud snoring for better than a half-hour, and then I rose.

I shuffled into the bathroom and looked at myself in the mirror. The guy looking back at me was middle-aged, slightly overweight, balding, and his eyes were bloodshot and puffy. When, I wondered, did this middle-aged guy move into my body?

I ran a hand over my head, examining the unaccustomed smoothness of the short cut. Up until the surgery, I had always worn my hair longer, somehow laboring under the illusion that by keeping it long I would be able to stave off the balding process. Of course the brain surgery had required my head being shaved, and since then I had opted to keep it short. Low maintenance. And a reminder that the old things had passed away—I was living in a new world now.

I wandered down the hall to the extra bedroom, which Ping used as something like an office. There was a desk, two chairs, and some bookshelves. I began searching the shelves for something to read.

This was a routine I was becoming more and more familiar with now that I had stopped sleeping altogether. Television struck me as mindless, and I had to do something to while away the hours between midnight and dawn. So I had taken to reading—and in the past few weeks, I had read almost as many books as I had in my entire college career.

I found a volume called "Undaunted Courage," by Stephen Ambrose, which was a history of the Lewis & Clark expedition, and I settled onto the living room sofa. I read until the sun came up, nearly finishing the book. Until my unique affliction, I had never been able to bring myself to read for more than a few minutes at a time. Now, with nothing else to do, hours melted away while I was reading. I took little pleasure in it, though—but without something to occupy my mind, I would have gone crazy.

When I heard the first birds of the day, I went to the kitchen and made coffee. I found the frying pan and did a quick survey of Ping's refrigerator—he had bacon, cheese, tomato, and eggs. There was bread in the cupboard, but no toaster to be found. I toasted bread in the oven's broiler, and made tomato and cheese omelets. I was just setting the bacon into the frying pan when Ping shuffled into the kitchen.

"Times have changed," he said. "I don't think you ever woke up before me in the old days."

He looked at the clock above the stove, and raised an eyebrow. It was 5:30.

I shrugged.

"I couldn't sleep," I said, pouring us some coffee. There was no cream or milk, but that was fine. I preferred mine black and from what I remembered so did Ping.

He sat down at the table and sipped his coffee while I set the food out. We ate without talking, with the speed of men who have either served in the armed forces or served time in prison.

I stood and started clearing the plates. Ping helped me wash the dishes in his sink. Ping told me he thought an automatic dishwasher would have been a waste of valuable capital.

We each drew off another hot cup of coffee, left the dishes to dry in the drainer, and went to the front porch. The sunlight illuminated the fog surrounding the house, but we couldn't see much beyond the first few trees at the edge of the lawn.

"So," Ping said at last.

"So," I said.

He slurped some coffee. "What makes you think you can do it?"

I didn't answer right away. Finally, I said, "Because I must do it."

He nodded.

"What makes you think I will help you?"

I looked at him without blinking.

"Because you once told me you owed me your life, and I believe you are a man who takes such things seriously."

He seemed to consider this, and then said, "Quinn, you're in no kind of shape to try something like this."

"I know."

"And there's a good chance we can't even find the guy."

"I know where he lives. He shouldn't be hard to track down."

"And we probably won't be able to get away with it."

"That doesn't matter to me."

Ping nodded and set down his coffee cup, leaning forward in his chair and drawing his fingers together like a steeple. I noticed that his fingers were thick and stubby, and looked like the fingers of an older man. I don't know why I had never noticed it before.

"What you're talking about is illegal," he said. "It's murder."

I set my own coffee cup down, and stood up. Ping didn't move, he just looked up at me and studied my face.

"Ping, my old friend, I am going to kill this man. I don't care that I might get caught, I don't care that it's illegal. The law means little to me now. I don't believe it is murder, but that's just my opinion. The bottom line is I am going to kill him, with or without your help."

Ping said nothing.

"So are you in or out?"

He smiled, and stood up.

"If you're serious," he said, "I will help you."

I was relieved—I had been counting on Ping's help and had been very afraid he wouldn't want to give it.

"I'm dead serious," I said.

He put his hands on my shoulders and looked me in the eyes.

"Quinn, once we start down this road, there is no turning back."

I felt a tear run down my cheek.

"Turning back ceased to be an option the day Angie died," I said.

Chapter 7

I spent the next night at home, cleaning a large amount of dog urine from my kitchen floor. I met Ping the following morning to start our planning and preparation. Ping figured he would be my coach, and I would do what he told me; that seemed to make a lot of sense to me, so that's the way we did it.

"Four phases to this operation," he said. "First, we need to get you into physical shape. That's going to take at least two months of hard training, maybe more. You don't need to be ready to do fifteen rounds at the Golden Gloves, but we at least need to get you toned up and solid. Any way you slice it, though, it's going to be late August before you're physically up to the job."

I didn't say anything and I wasn't going to interrupt him.

"Second, we have to start watching this cat, figure out his habits, and look for our opportunities."

"Third, we make a plan. This whole operation has to be carefully planned, and it has to go by the numbers."

"Finally, well, that one should be self-explanatory."

Ping added: "Maybe you don't care if we get caught, but I do. And that's good too, because one of us does need to care. We'll take this guy down, but it's wrong if we go down with him. That's not justice. So," he said, smiling, "my plan is that we put him away, and we walk free."

That was fine with me, but not important. I didn't want Ping to end up in prison of course, but I wasn't concerned about my own freedom, as long as Danny Minor paid for what he had done. Paid with his life.

"You're running this like it's a mission," I said.

He shrugged.

"Is this the kind of thing you've been doing since you got out?" I asked.

Ping looked directly into my eyes, but said nothing. My turn to shrug.

We started my training that afternoon with a one-mile run down the state highway. By the time I reached the end of the mile, I was out of breath, my right side felt like someone had put a spear in it, my head felt like it was going to explode, and I was ready to puke.

"You taking to this very well, honorable Mister Black," Ping said in his best just-off-the-rice-paddy accent.

I was bent over, elbows on my knees, trying to catch my breath. I waved an arm at him, which of course he understood to mean, "Shut the hell up."

I stood up, and sweat rolled into my eyes, stinging slightly. The sun shone so bright it hurt. This was going to be harder than I had thought, and Ping was right: I was in no shape to do this thing I had decided to do.

I looked at him, standing there in his gray sweats and white tee shirt. He hadn't even broken a sweat.

"How long 'til I'm ready, do you think?" I asked between gasps.

Ping shook his head.

"No use talking about it," he said. Then he sprinted off, calling back over his shoulder, "Let's run, Marine!"

I ran.

The first day was not the worst—I'd say the worst was the

third day. We were running along Meecham Road, Ping with the easy gate of a man who is running nowhere near his capacity and me with sweat soaking my tee shirt. I was breathing hard, and the grade of the incline began to increase. The sun on my back started to feel like a hot iron being pressed against my flesh, but I kept running. Ping began to pull ahead, and he turned around and jogged backwards, facing me and smiling.

"C'mon, round-eye! You'll never get the job done like this! Focus!"

He turned and sprinted and was over the top of the hill and gone.

Cars went by, leaving a gust of hot July wind and kerosene-like smell in their wake.

Suddenly, my head was spinning and I felt the urge to puke. I stopped, putting my hands on my knees and bending way over, trying to get blood flowing to my head. The problem was, I didn't stop bending over—I just kept going, and my head slammed into the ground. Everything dissolved into a shower of golden sparks, and then it was quiet and dark.

I woke gasping for breath. I couldn't see. I was on my back. I rolled over, and opened my eyes. The reason I couldn't breath was that I was vomiting. Someone's hand was pressed firmly against my forehead, and for a moment I thought it was Angie, because that's what she would do when I was sick.

Ping said, "At least you didn't die."

Not Angie, then.

Reality came rushing back.

I finished vomiting and rolled to a sitting position. I was just off the sidewalk, still next to the road. Ping must have carried me there when he saw I had passed out.

I put up a hand indicating I didn't want to talk. Ping nodded and I just sat there, breathing. My head hurt, and my mouth tasted bitter and salty. I could feel that my lip was busted. My right shoulder felt like someone had smacked it with a Louisville Slugger.

Finally, I stood up. Ping stood too, but said nothing.

"Well, I can't quit at least until I make it over the top," I said.

Ping nodded and we ran.

It was a Saturday morning that only the Chamber of Commerce could have dreamed up—temperature about seventy-eight, bright blue sky with a few big white puffy clouds, and a pleasant breeze blowing. You couldn't order a better day in late August.

I had worked my way up to a seven-mile run each day in a little over a month. But today we were not running. We had lifted weights in Ping's garage earlier in the morning, and Ping was reviewing the finer points of hand-to-hand combat with me. It was something I had learned in the Corps, and I had quickly filed it away as finished and forgotten when I became a civilian advertising salesman.

Ping, on the other had, had always relished fighting, and had become something of a hero in our unit after winning the division championships for boxing two times in a row.

"Boxing is too narrow," he was saying to me now. "It's about punching, which is not how most fights go. Most fights end up on the ground."

He stepped forward, and I raised my fists. The next thing I knew I was lying on my back—he had swept a leg behind my feet and pushed on my chest, and I hit the ground before I knew what was happening. I smiled.

"How'd I do?"

Ping shook his head.

"We'll hope you're a better shot than you are a fighter."

This was beginning to annoy me. I got up.

"Let's go again," I said.

Chapter 8

Dr. Bibbs was shaking his head as I was buttoning up my shirt. He sat on the little stool in the examination room, tapping the end of his stethoscope on the palm of his left hand. Good thing he had the foresight to take out the earpieces first, I thought.
I hopped off the exam table and tucked in my shirt, and then I sat back down. The paper sheets on the table made a lot of noise. "I don't know what to tell you, Quinn," he said.
"Am I okay?" I asked.

He nodded.

"You seem to be," he said. I refused to believe it of him, but for just a moment he almost seemed disappointed.

"By all we know," he said, "you shouldn't be okay—hell, Quinn, you shouldn't even be alive. But I can't find a damn thing wrong with you."

He picked up my chart from the counter top and flipped through it page by page.

"I can't find a single thing that distinguishes you from any other healthy 35-year-old."

He flipped the chart closed and tossed it back onto the counter.

"And what about these weird episodes I've been having?" I asked.

He shook his head. "I don't know, Quinn."

He glanced at my face.

"I know that isn't a very satisfactory answer, but that's all I have for you at this point."

Neither of us said anything for a while.

"Then I should just not worry about it?" I said.

He turned his palms upward and shrugged.

"That approach seems to be working so far," he said.

It was amazing to think I was paying him for this advice. Ping had been telling me the same thing for weeks, and he didn't charge me.

Of course, knowing I shouldn't worry about something and actually being able to stop worrying were two very different things.

Chapter 9

I sold the house.

It might have been a cowardly thing to do—sometimes I believe that is just what it was, cowardly—but I really couldn't bear it any more. Every time I walked in the door, I was reliving that night. I would sometimes just stand in the kitchen and weep. It was as if the death lived on in the house, just lingering and waiting for me to come in the door, as real as those early morning Northwest fogs which make Spokane's airport one of the most-often-fogged-in the country, right up there with San Francisco.

I found a comfortable little apartment on Baker Street, in a small building owned by Francis Hudson. Mrs. Hudson was a widow, wife of the former Doctor Richard Hudson. She was, as near as I could tell, about eighty years old, but as energetic as most forty-year-olds. The apartment building had once been home for her and Doc Hudson—back when Baker Street was still a fashionable address. Nowadays, the neighborhood was filled with rental houses, young people just starting out or old people just winding down.

I liked it just fine.

Probably what cinched the deal was Powder.

I was looking the apartment over, and Mrs. Hudson was showing me around.

"We had a bathroom for every bedroom upstairs," she said. I looked over my shoulder at her—something in her voice made me want to check and make sure she was all right—and caught her with a wistful look on her face.

She noticed I was looking at her and she smiled.

"We entertained a lot in those days, Mr. Black. People don't do that much anymore, do they?"

"I don't know, Mrs. Hudson. Angie and I didn't do much entertaining," I said, "but then we didn't have a house quite so large."

She smiled again.

"We didn't either, when we started out, young man."

I bowed, conceding the point.

The apartment was really quite amazing. There was a small living room, a bedroom of enormous proportions, a bathroom complete with a tub and shower, and off the living room a small kitchenette. There were furnishings in the Victorian style, including a bed and a sofa and chair —but none of it was too stuffy-looking. There was a fireplace in the living room.

I sat on the sofa and looked up at Mrs. Hudson.

"There is one small matter," I said.

"The dog?"

Now it was my turn to smile.

"You saw him?"

"He was rather hard to miss, Mr. Black. I think perhaps you should rescue him from your car, and we can talk about him on the front porch."

Who was I to argue with a lady?

We stepped into the wide hallway, walked down the steps, and Mrs. Hudson waited on the porch while I retrieved Powder from the Blazer. He seemed to have been catapulted from the vehicle as soon as I opened the door, and he flew across the lawn in a blur of flapping ears and stubby legs. I watched as Mrs. Hudson sat in the great porch swing, and Powder leapt into her lap.

I walked across the lawn to the porch—somewhat less enthusiastically than Powder, I admit—and I noticed Mrs. Hudson scratching Powder behind the ears. My plan was unfolding perfectly, I thought.

I sat on the swing next to them. Powder looked at me curiously but did not move from Mrs. Hudson's lap. After all, when you had a good backrub going, why interrupt it?

Mrs. Hudson looked at me, tilting her head slightly downward and gazing at me from under her eyebrows. It was almost as if she were accustomed to wearing reading glasses and glancing over the top of them, like a school librarian.

"Mr. Black, you wouldn't be engaging in blatant manipulation, now would you?"

"Absolutely."

"And you suppose that simply because the dog is adorable and loving, that I might relent on my 'no pets' policy?"

"That was part of the plan, yes."

She now raised the eyebrows.

"Part of the plan? And what is the *rest* of the plan?"

"Well, Mrs. Hudson, I was also hoping that you might agree to help take care of Powder when I'm away."

She said nothing, but proceeded to use both hands to gently rub Powder's shoulders. He settled his head between his paws, closed his eyes, and heaved a deep sigh. Doggy heaven.

"You plan to be away a lot, Mr. Black?"

I nodded.

"Yes, I have my physical therapy, and something else I'm working on that is taking up a lot of my time."

Now she was silent. Across the street, a young couple in their early twenties got into a rusty Chevy Cavalier and pulled away from the curb in a haze of blue smoke. They had no idea how lucky they were, I thought. No idea at all.

"Does that hurt?" Mrs. Hudson asked.

I realized I was rubbing the scar on the back of my head.

"Sometimes," I said. "Sometimes more than others. I can live with it. It's not the worst pain I've ever had."

She nodded.

"It would be nice to have someone here more often," she said. "And you seem like a nice man."

I didn't answer. I could have, but somehow I would have felt dishonest—after all, I was planning to kill someone—so I said nothing.

"I could pay you extra for taking care of the dog," I offered.

She smiled again.

"Very well," she said. "I will agree, on one condition."

"Which is?"

"That you agree to have dinner with me every now and then," she said.

"I think I can accept those terms," I said.

She nodded and continued to rub absently at the back of Powder's neck. He offered no objections. We sat there for quite some time. It was quite pleasant—people should do it more often.

Moving day was not much to write home about. I sold most of the stuff from the house in an estate sale. I hired a guy named Pete Bendy ("Pete's Auctions!") to handle it for me. It was easy to decide what to sell. I just put the few things I wanted to keep in the back of the Blazer. One of those things was Angie's laptop computer. I had been reading through some of her emails, and discovered that some of them were encrypted. I didn't know the password. I didn't even know why Angie might have encrypted emails on her computer. I was planning to take the computer to a friend of mine who thought he could unlock the encryption.

I closed the Blazer door, turned to Pete, and told him to sell the rest of the stuff in the house.

"Everything?" he asked.

"Everything."

He was still staring at me, so I handed him the keys to the house.

"Pete, when I come back, I want the house empty and ready to sell. I don't want to see anything left."

Then I got in my truck and drove away. He was still staring after me as I turned the corner.

I drove straight to the apartment and started carrying the few boxes upstairs. I had kept enough of the dishes to feed a guest and me, a few of my favorite CD's, some books, and my clothes. I put the laptop on the kitchen counter, stopping to stare at it briefly. The emails were bugging me. A lot. I returned to the task of unpacking.

I had kept all our pictures and videos. I knew there would be nights when I would bring those out and wallow in self-pity. For now I stored them in the top of the closet.

Powder watched all this from the comfort of the bed, his tail wagging the whole time. He cocked his head to one side, sprang from the bed, and ran out the bedroom door.

When I walked back into the living room, Ping was there, sitting on my sofa. Powder was at his feet, tail wagging.

"Nice place," Ping said.

"It'll do."

"Got any beer?"

I shook my head.

"Good thing I brought some, then," he said.

He got up and went over to the fridge, and when he opened it I saw that the only thing inside was a case of Amber Ale.

"Why bother asking if you already knew?" I said.

"Seems proper to ask," Ping said. He pulled out two bottles, tossed one to me, and we sat down and opened them up.

Powder looked from me to Ping, and then settled on the

sofa next to Ping. Damn dog.

I sat in the armchair, and took a long drink of the beer.

"Warm," I said.

"Ingrate," Ping said.

Powder huffed, as if adding his own comment. Ping and I looked at each other, then at Powder. I shrugged.

"So," Ping said after a while.

"So."

"I have some ideas about how this ought to go."

I feigned surprise and puzzlement.

"How what ought to go?"

Ping finished his beer and got up to get another one.

"Operation Justice, what else?"

Ping handed me another beer, too, and I set it down on the coffee table because I hadn't finished the first one yet.

Ping sat down.

"Want to hear?"

I nodded.

"We finish up with your rehab within the next week or so. You're almost ready now, but another week wouldn't hurt. Meanwhile, we can start trailing Danny Minor. We need to make a study of him. Learn his habits, who his buddies are, when we can most likely find him alone."

Ping waited, as if he expected me to say something. When he realized I wasn't going to, he continued.

"We need to spend at least a week or two watching him," Ping said. "We want to pick up the patterns, make sure we're not missing something."

I finished the first beer, set it down, and twisted the top off the second one.

"Like what?" I said.

"Like a friend that's watching his back or a neighbor that might see us, or even a certain police detective that might also be watching Minor."

That made sense.

"And then?" I asked.

Ping took a drink of his beer.

"And then, when we're sure, we kill him."

That sounded fine to me, so I just drank my beer and said nothing.

Finally, Ping said softly, "Doesn't that bother you just a little, Quinn?"

I sipped my beer.

"Only a little"

He said nothing.

"I know it sounds cold. But all I have to do is think about Angie lying on that floor."

"I know," Ping said. He appeared to be searching for something down the neck of his beer bottle. Finally he looked up at me. "I just have to be sure."

"Sure of what? Me?"

He nodded.

"Quinn, this is a serious thing we're talking about doing. I have no problem doing it—some people need to be killed. That's my opinion. If I'm the one who needs to do the killing, I also have no problem with that."

I waited.

"But?"

"But Quinn, you're different from me."

"Different how?"

"You believe in God."

I set my beer down. This was something unexpected.

"What do you mean?"

"Just what I said, Quinn. You believe in God. The God who said, 'Thou shalt not kill.' I'm worried that you are not going to be able to carry this through—and I don't want to find that out at the wrong moment. It could get both of us killed."

I nodded.

"You're worried I might get us shot?"

He shrugged, which meant of course he was worried about that.

"The God I once believed in will not stand in our way," I said.

I could see something in his eyes.

"What?"

"The God you 'once believed in?'"

I finished my beer and got up for another one.

"That God will have no problem with what we are about to do."

Powder huffed, as if he agreed.

Chapter 10

The next day I found an old postcard in one of the boxes I had kept. In 1997, Angie and I had gone to Mexico, and she had sent the card from Mazatlan—she had sent it to herself. I remember her telling me it was to help with what she called "Post Mexican Depression."

I sat on the bed looking at the postcard. Powder came trotting into the bedroom and sat at my feet, looking up at me with his head cocked to one side. His eyes were revealed nothing, but they seemed to twinkle. I wondered, not for the first time, if Powder experienced any of the moods or emotions I attributed to him, or if I was a victim of anthropomorphism. I leaned toward Powder and said in a whisper, "Would you like a biscuit?"

He leapt to all fours and began whirling in a circle, yapping at the top of his lungs and wagging his tail.

To hell with anthropomorphism. This was a happy dog.

I walked to the kitchen to get Powder a dog biscuit, and stuck the postcard to the fridge with a magnet.

Chapter 11

Father Michael O'Dell was the priest who lived just down the street from Mrs. Hudson's apartment building. He was something of an anomaly—big, muscular, and always smiling. Not what I thought of when I thought of priests.

I saw him each morning, taking his jog, and then usually in the evenings on his way back from the church. St. Vincent's was only three blocks away, and that was apparently where he worked. Or pastored. Or whatever it is they do.

I am not Catholic. My parents were Methodist and I stopped attending church altogether when I went to college.

Angie and I had gone to church occasionally, usually on Easter and Christmas. But today I found myself wanting to talk with Father O'Dell. My conversation with Ping had left me more than a little disturbed, though I would never let Ping know that.

I walked into the front door of St. Vincent's at about eight o'clock on a Tuesday night. It was an old church—the kind they don't build anymore. I looked at the high ceilings, the intricate moldings and detailing that covered every square inch, and the stained glass depiction of the Passion of Christ and wondered how much money had been spent to build the place. I also wondered what Christ would have thought of it. After all, he hadn't spent any of his money building immense churches—in fact, he said something about giving everything to the poor.

"You're about an hour late," Father O'Dell said. He was standing beside me. I was a little bothered that I had not seen him when I came in. So much for my cat-like reflexes.

"Late for what?"

He gestured toward the pews.

"For Mass," he said. "It was at seven."

He was taller than me, by a good three inches. I wondered if he had ever played football.

"I wanted to talk," I said.

I felt suddenly stupid, like a little boy who didn't know what to say to his dad. I suppose that's why they make you call them "Father"—it puts you on the defensive. Of course it doesn't hurt if the Father happens to be six-foot-four.

"About religion," I said. "About God."

He just nodded. He walked to the last pew, and motioned with an open palm toward it.

"Why don't we sit?" he said.

I looked around the sanctuary, to see if there was anyone else I had missed.

He smiled.

"There's nobody else here," he said. "Your secrets are safe with me."

Somehow I had imagined we would be sitting in his office—he behind a big oak desk. Instead, we were here in the empty sanctuary, sitting side-by-side. I think I would have preferred the barrier of the oak desk.

"My name is Michael O'Dell," he said.

"I know."

I took a deep breath. Why the hell was I so nervous? I wasn't even Catholic.

"My name is Black. Quinn Black."

He said nothing.

"Father, do you believe in Jesus?"

It came out of me quietly, almost a whisper, and in the chasm of the sanctuary it seemed a supremely ridiculous question to ask a priest. If there had been a rock handy, I would have gladly crawled underneath it.

"That depends," Father O'Dell said. He was matching my quiet tone. They probably taught them that at priest school.

"Do you mean the historical Jesus? The religion of Jesus? Or the religion about Jesus?"

I thought about this. He had matched my strange question with one of his own.

"Jesus who forgives everything," I said. "Jesus who said to turn the other cheek."

He was looking at his fingernails.

"Jesus who let criminals and thieves brutally murder him," I said.

He kept studying his fingernails. They must have been extraordinary in some way that escaped me.

"Ah, that Jesus," he said. "Now that is a tough one."

He looked at me.

"Do you mind if I ask why you're asking? After all, I am a priest. Most people would assume I believed in Jesus."

I laughed.

"Presumptuous of me, wasn't it?" I said.

He was still looking at me.

"No, not really. But unusual, yes. I don't think I've ever been asked that question by one of my flock."

"I'm sorry Father. I'm not Catholic."

He smiled.

"That's all right, Quinn. I still consider you one of my flock." He paused, and then more quietly said, "Now, why would you be asking a priest if he believes in Jesus?"

"I'm having a hard time forgiving, Father. A very hard time."

He said nothing.

"And a hard time understanding why God allows terrible things to happen to innocent people."

"Yes," he said. "I see. That is a difficult issue, Quinn Black. I struggle with that one myself."

"You?"

He laughed now.

"Yes, me. Is that so hard to believe? After all, I have spent many years thinking about these things. More time than most people. I spent three years in Viet Nam with the Army. I saw things there I wouldn't have imagined possible. And I asked myself, how can God allow this to happen to His children?"

I waited. I suppose I expected him to spout the answer out and solve one of the world's oldest theological questions, right here in St. Vincent's, at eight o'clock on a Tuesday.

"And what kind of answer did you come up with, Father?"

He shook his head.

"Still working on it."

I was disappointed.

"I've read Aquinas," I said. "I've read Barth, Kung, and Brunner. I don't know that I have found anyone who could answer this question for me. I'm sorry to have troubled you. It was a shot in the dark."

I started to get up, but he placed his hand on my arm. It was a big hand. I sat back down.

"You've read all these theologians?"

"Yes," I said, "but just from a layman's perspective. And only recently. So I'm still trying to sort it all out in my mind."

He was looking at me with more interest now.

"Recently?"

I cleared my throat.

"Yes, within the last month."

He said nothing, and I realized my mistake. They were, after all, big books.

"I don't sleep much," I said.

He let go of my arm and said, "I should say not."

"I have this idea, Quinn Black, that maybe God doesn't interfere in these cases because He can't."

"He can't?"

"Right. Has it ever occurred to you that perhaps God set the universe in motion and then allowed it to play out without His interference?"

I nodded.

"Yes, it has. But what about miracles then? What about the feeding of the five thousand, or the parting of the Red Sea? Or Jesus rising from the dead?"

He put his hands on the back of the pew in front of him.

"Yes, those do present a problem for my theory," he said at last. "Perhaps they were exaggerated."

"But, Father, if they didn't really happen, what does that make of our religion?"

He smiled.

"I asked you before, Quinn Black—the religion of Jesus, or the religion about Jesus?"

"I'm not sure."

"Neither am I," he said. "That's why I am still here, doing this job."

There was a fluttering of wings and for a moment it occurred to me that perhaps an angel had been eavesdropping on our conversation—but as I looked up I saw a pigeon moving from one rafter to another above us. Father O'Dell didn't comment on this, but I wondered how many pigeon droppings they had to clean off the pews because of their uninvited guest.

"The only other explanation is, I'm afraid, somewhat unsatisfying," he said.

"And what is that explanation?"

"That everything happens for a reason."

My mind screamed. How I hated these words. What could have been the reason for Angie's suffering? What kind of God would demand such a thing?

"I can see that you have considered this before," O'Dell said. "But consider it again. Consider the idea that we might be not be able to understand all of God's purposes—because we are not God."

Well, at last he had started talking like a priest. I was disappointed, but not surprised. It was bound to have happened sooner or later.

"Wait," he said. "Before you dismiss me, I ask you to think about something."

I waited.

"You are no doubt thinking that this business of us not being able to understand is a cop-out."

"Well, yes, that is exactly what I was thinking."

He was looking at the pigeon now, high above us on a rafter.

"Tell me, Quinn, is the pigeon able to understand mathematics?"

"What?"

"Mathematics. You and I both acknowledge the reality of mathematics. We know mathematics explain the physical world perfectly. Correct?"

This was interesting, because in all my reading I had not encountered this line of thought. Of course, though I had read a lot, I had not read everything.

"Yes," I said. "Of course you are correct."

He gestured to the pigeon.

"But does the pigeon have any chance of ever understanding mathematics?"

"No, of course not."

"Correct. The pigeon doesn't have the equipment—the brain capacity—to understand."

"But, Father, we are not pigeons."

He smiled at me now.

"No?"

I shook my head.

"Not even to God?"

I had no answer to this.

"Quinn, we humans are an arrogant lot. Since we have reason and self-awareness, we seem to think we are capable of knowing anything and everything. Does that sound like a description of any being you might have heard of before? A being that knows anything and everything?"

I swallowed.

"God."

"Yes. And do you believe that if humans try hard enough—if we have an attitude that is positive enough—if we build a fast enough computer—that we will ever become God?"

"No."

"Then doesn't it follow that, like the pigeon, there may be some things we simply may not be able to understand? And that even though we can't conceive them, these things are still true?"

"Yes, Father. But the pigeon example isn't fair."

He raised an eyebrow.

"And why not?"

"Because," I said, "there is no morality in mathematics."

I thought I had him.

"But how do you know, Quinn?"

I had no answer.

"So," I said, "we are back where we started."

He leaned a little closer.

"Quinn, tell me—have you ever seen mathematics?"

"Well of course I have," I said, getting a little irritated. He had his favorite argument, and he was going to stick with it, I guess.

"No, no, no!" he said, seeming as irritated as I was, "you're not listening. You have seen the symbols in a math book perhaps, but have you ever seen mathematics itself."

"No," I said.

"Then why do you believe in it?" he asked.

"Because it explains so much of the world," I said, "And there is a lot of evidence to support it."

He leaned back.

"That is why I believe in God, Quinn."

"Faith," I said.

"Faith."

"You believe that everything happens for a purpose, even if we don't understand it," I asked.

"I choose to believe this, yes," he said.

"And we are always working toward God's purpose?"

"Yes."

"Even Hitler?"

He said nothing.

"I withdraw the question," I said.

There was, after all, no reason to be mean about it.

"No, no, Quinn," he said, and I could hear a genuine note of concern in his voice. "That's the one thing you must not do. You must never withdraw the question. Then you really are no better off than the pigeon."

We sat for a while, and I noticed for the first time that the candles burning at the front of the church were really quite beautiful.

When I got up to leave, Father O'Dell didn't move.

I don't know if he was praying, or if he had fallen asleep.

I don't suppose it matters.

Chapter 12

It was Wednesday, and Ping and I decided to spend some time watching Danny Minor. We knew we were risking a lost evening—after all, Danny might have been in church for Wednesday night prayer meeting—but being daredevils, we were up for the risk. Anyway, what else is there to do on a Wednesday night in October?

It was chilly. The leaves were fluttering at the ends of the branches, many of them brown or bright yellow, but not too many falling just yet.

Minor lived in an area of town called Peaceful Valley. It's anything but peaceful.

Peaceful Valley is northwest of downtown, in a valley near the river, below the railroad tracks and the interstate. Most of the houses here might have been nice forty years ago but now struggle to stand upright under the weight of too many coats of paint, decades of deterioration, and the occasional refrigerator on the front porch.

Ping and I were sitting in his truck, about two blocks down from Minor's house. The truck windows were fogged from the cups of coffee we had sitting on the dash, but not so fogged that we couldn't see out. Ping had the darkest kind of tinting on his truck windows, and the combination of steam and window tint would have made it impossible for anyone to see who was sitting inside the truck—or even if anyone were inside at all.

Ping reached inside his jacket and pulled out a gun—gleaming dully in the streetlight I could see it was a Glock, like the one I had tried to buy at the pawnshop. He held it out to me. Then I realized it wasn't just any Glock—it was the Glock.

"I knew you loved it," he said.

I shrugged and took the gun. It felt good in my hands. I checked the clip and the chamber. A full load.

I reached inside my own jacket to retrieve the .38 Ping had given me to use, and he shook his head.

"You keep it for now," he said. "You might need it."

I tucked the Glock inside my belt and pulled my jacket back over it.

"They wouldn't issue me a permit," I said.

"I know."

"Guess they were afraid I might shoot somebody," I said.

"I'm sure that's what they were thinking."

We sat and watched.

We had been sitting there with the engine off for more than three hours. It was cold in the truck. We were down to the last two cups of coffee, so I was estimating we would only last another hour or so. I desperately needed to pee.

So far, we had seen nothing. I mean nothing at all—nobody had come in or out of the little clapboard house. There was a light on in the upstairs bedroom, but the curtain was drawn. We had seen no shadows or movement, but that didn't mean anything—maybe Minor was lying on the bed, catching up on his Shakespeare or Spinoza.

"Are you sure this is the right house?" I asked.

Ping sighed through his nose.

"Of course I'm sure. I double-checked the address. I've seen him here myself."

I sipped my coffee loudly. Still managed to burn my

tongue. I hate it when I do that. Nothing would taste right for two days.

We sat for a while longer.

"You don't suppose he's had a heart attack up there, do you?"

Ping didn't answer.

"I mean, I would really be disappointed if I didn't get to kill him."

Pig set his coffee cup back on the dash.

"You only make jokes because you're afraid," he said.

He didn't look at me—he just continued staring at the house.

"Yes," I said.

Ping nodded.

"The jokes are funnier because they're true," I said.

He nodded again.

"I don't think you—"

Ping put a hand on my shoulder and I stopped talking. A person was walking by my side of the truck. Ping must have seen them in the rear-view mirror.

It was a man, walking slowly but with a steady, deliberate gate. He didn't slow down as he passed the truck. He was wearing a hooded blue sweatshirt. Across the back it read "Wolverines" in white letters.

"Danny Minor," Ping whispered.

I froze.

"You sure?"

Ping looked at me now, and though I couldn't read the expression on his face in the darkness, I could see the streetlight glint in his eyes. He was focused, intent. Studying me. Waiting for a reaction.

"Quinn, do not get out of the car."

I couldn't breathe. All I could do was watch Minor walk up the front porch steps of his house. My body was suddenly coiled with the tension of my muscles. I was flexing and unflexing my fists.

I took a deep, slow breath.

"I'm fine," I said. "I'm not going to do anything stupid."

Ping didn't move.

His hand was still on my arm. His eyes were still searching for a hint of movement from me.

I nodded toward the house.

"Look," I said.

Two men were coming out of the house. They were both carrying guns, holding them low and close to their bodies, but not troubling to hide them.

"Not hiding them at all," I whispered.

"They want us to see them," Ping said.

I turned to look at him again.

"Did he see us?"

Ping shook his head.

"I don't think so," he said. "But I think he believes we are watching him. Or that we might be. Or at least that *somebody* might be."

"So the guns and the other two guys are a warning?"

"Yeah. Show of strength."

Minor was talking to the two men. His back was to the street, but the two with the guns were watching over his shoulder, looking up and down the street, between the parked cars, pausing now and then to look into a shadowy area and then move on. They seemed practiced at it.

One of them looked right at me. Or it seemed like it—actually it was only a second, as he was sweeping the street with his gaze, but for a split second I could have sworn he was looking at me.

One of the men was a tall black man, very muscular, with a completely shaven head. The other was white, stockier, with a short haircut. Regulation.

"Marines?"

Ping grunted.

"Don't think so," he said. "Wannabes. Look at the way they're holding their weapons. They know what they're doing, but they don't look like they were trained at Paris Island."

"You can tell that by looking?" I asked.

"No, but it's funny to know you would buy it."

He chuckled.

A third man came onto the porch. He said something to the other two, and they walked to the opposite ends of the porch and stood in the shadows. I could now barely make them out—and only because I already knew they were there. Someone approaching the house probably would have missed them completely. We were about to see this was the idea. We were witnessing some kind of a meeting. Most likely they didn't know we were watching them at all—most likely they thought one of their underworld rivals might be.

The new man—dressed slightly better in a sweater and dark jeans—put his arm around Minor's shoulder, and they both faced the street as they talked. They appeared to be waiting for someone.

After a few minutes, a black Honda Accord pulled up to the curb directly in front of the house. Stupid. He should've parked down the street and walked. Pulling up front like that was very dramatic, but it gave no element of surprise.

I didn't know exactly what was going on, but if it was all friendly and nice, one wouldn't position armed goons at either end of the porch waiting for a guest of honor.

The back door of the Honda opened, and a man in a suit got out. I couldn't see his face.

He walked up the steps and said something to Minor and the other man.

Minor snapped his fingers, and the goons stepped out of the shadows, their guns in hand. The man in the suit looked from left to right, and then appeared to laugh.

"Minor doesn't seem amused," Ping said. He was right. Danny Minor seemed more agitated than ever. He shouted something and jabbed the man in the sweater with his index finger. This irritated the man.

The goons moved closer, and then all six men went in the front door of the house. The door closed.

Ping picked up his coffee and slurped it.

"Interesting," he said.

I said nothing.

"We don't really know if he has more firepower inside the house or not."

I shrugged, and then realized Ping couldn't see me. So much for being prosaic.

"We could have shot him as he walked by, pulled away, and they wouldn't have known what hit him," I said.

"That's exactly what we could not do," Ping said.

He was looking at me again, and his eyes were set in that squint of his—the disapproval squint is how I think of it. If I had been able to see his mouth, his lips would have been pressed together, and his nostrils slightly flared. It was the look he would give to our C.O. back in the Gulf, usually after college-boy had made an unusually idiotic statement.

"And why not?"

Ping set his coffee cup back down and sighed.

"Because the aim is to take him out, not to go out with him."

I said nothing.

"And not to get caught. The justice system, which failed you so miserably, would also have no qualms about grinding you under its wheels."

"I don't care about that, Ping."

"I know. That's why it's my job to care for both of us."

"Why?"

"For starters, because I don't want to go to prison."

That seemed reasonable on his part.

"You don't have to do this, then," I said.

"Yes, I do. Because you're my friend. Because I owe you from the Gulf. And because it's the right thing to do."

"Then—"

He put a hand on my shoulder again.

"And it's also the right thing to keep us both out of prison. Trust me; you don't want to be in there. As bad as you have been hurt, going to prison will not make it better."

That made some sense, so I kept quiet.

"And Quinn, Angie wouldn't want you going to prison for the sake of this douche bag."

I swallowed hard.

"Would she?" he said.

"No."

Ping nodded.

It was quiet in the cab of the truck. So quiet I could hear my pulse thumping in my ears. I had a flash of that hyper-real feeling from before—the cab of the truck seemed vast to me, too large, too real. I could feel a sense of panic coming on. I drew in my breath quickly and grabbed onto the dash of the truck.

"What?"

Ping sat forward and looked alarmed. His hand went under his jacket—I knew he had gripped the butt of his own weapon.

"No, no, it's nothing," I said. He seemed to relax a little.

"I have these moments," I said. "Moments of—I don't know, a surge of adrenaline, maybe."

Ping studied my face as if he were trying to take in more light in the dimness of the cab.

"Maybe I'm going crazy," I said finally. "I haven't been sleeping."

Ping nodded.

"You told me," he said.

"No. Not the whole truth."

"What do you mean?"

I took in a slow breath and tried to calm myself. The feeling of the chasm, of the terrifying sense of space, was passing. I looked at the house for a moment—no movement there. Nothing happening.

Ping leaned forward.

"How much sleep have you been getting?"

I cleared my throat.

"None," I said.

"None? As in zero?"

I nodded.

"For how many days?"

I swallowed.

"Since the hospital."

Ping was silent, but his gaze never left my face. Finally, he said, "Are you telling me you haven't slept in over five months?"

I said, "Yes."

"Not one hour?"

"That's what I'm telling you," I said.

He leaned back in his seat and exhaled long and slow.

"How is that possible?"

I told him all of it—everything the doctor had said to me, all that I had learned from my reading and my research. I told him that by all rights I should not still be functioning at all, but for some reason that neither I nor Dr. Bibbs could explain, I still was functioning.

"I think these panic attacks, or whatever they are, have something to do with my sleep problem. Or my no-sleep problem."

Ping shifted in his seat.

"I'm having a hard time with this one, Quinn."

I looked out the window.

"There's our boy," I said.

Minor was at the front door again. He was escorting the man in the suit down the steps and back out to the car. The other man followed, and the two goons were in back. Minor got into the car with the man in the suit, and they closed the door.

The car pulled away.

I reached for the ignition, but Ping put his hand on mine to stop me.

"They're watching the street for movement," he said.

He was right. The three men on the porch were looking up and down the street. They stood there until the Honda was out of site, and then they went back inside.

"Well," I said. "We lost him."

"True enough, my friend, but we have now learned that he's into something more than just run-of-the-mill burglary. And we know that he has quite a few well-armed friends."

"I suppose you're right."

"So," Ping said, "this mission was a success. We did what we came to do, which was to watch and learn."

I picked up my coffee and sipped it. It had gone cold.

"So now what?"

He sat back in his seat.

"We wait at least another half an hour, and then we start up the truck and leave."

CHAPTER 13

The next morning I telephoned Kim Lutrell, Angie's former boss at James, Kennedy, and Castle, Spokane's most affluent law firm. Kim had been Angie's supervisor in the paralegal department, and they had become good friends. Kim was a paralegal; Angie was working on her law degree. I wondered if Kim knew anything about the encrypted e-mail messages, but I didn't mention that in our brief telephone conversation. I just asked if we could meet in person.

Kim didn't want to meet at the office. I was relieved, because I didn't really much want to go there. I had visited Angie at her workplace many times. Going back there now would just lead to a lot of questions and uncomfortable conversations. We decided to meet at Starbucks at 5:15, after Kim finished work.

Kim arrived 15 minutes late. She probably got stuck at the office. Angie was always late like that, too. Kim sat across from me at a small table, fidgeting with her Chai Tea and looking nervous. But before I could ask her any questions, she said, "I shouldn't be talking to you at all, Quinn."

I took a sip of coffee.

"Why not?"

She sighed and slid a manila envelope across the table to me.

"Please don't open that here," she said.

"What's in it?"

"Documents about the Cerazini insurance fraud case. Angie had access to them."

"Was Angie in some kind of trouble?"

"Quinn, I'm sorry as hell for what happened. But this is all I can do for you. I've put my job in jeopardy as it is."

I took another drink of coffee, sat my coffee mug on the table, and looked around the store. There was a cute college couple huddled over a Macintosh computer; two old ladies who seemed to be sisters; and a guy in suit reading a copy of the paper.

"Angie was doing research on some of the Cerazini holdings," Kim said. "That's all I know."

Kim stood up.

"Quinn, please don't call me about any of this again. I just can't afford to lose my job, and I could for giving you that file. I'm sorry about what happened."

"Sure," I said. I didn't get up. "I understand, Kim."

She left without looking back. She hadn't touched her tea. I drank it, and opened the file.

"So what was in the file?" Ping said, wiping the sweat from his brow. We had just finished our workout. It was 8 p.m.

"Just a bunch of real estate deeds with the name of Cerazini's company on them, some public notices, some Polaroids of the properties. And police reports on a couple of fires."

He gulped some water.

"Was Angie looking up Cerazini's skirt?"

I stared at him.

"So to speak," he said.

"I still need to find out about those encrypted e-mails," I said. "Tomorrow morning I'm going to see a computer expert."

Robin Helton was a computer geek's computer geek.

He lived in a tidy bungalow on Mason Lane, near Central High School. I had met him a couple of years ago through Jay and Kevin, the morning deejays on one of the radio stations I worked for. Jay and Kevin were a bit of an oddity for Spokane radio. They worked for a country music station but played very little music on their show. They spent a lot of time in their boss's office trying to explain things they said on they air that generated complaints to the Federal Communications Commission .

Jay and Kevin also had some quirky guests. One of them was Robin Helton, who was known to listeners as "Mister Find Out Anything." I had called Jay and Kevin's producer Bob Castle to get Robin's phone number.

I knocked on Robin's door and heard someone inside shout, "It's open."

I pushed and the door swung wide.

Robin was hanging upside down from the ceiling, like a bat. He even seemed to have wings drooping from his shoulders.

My eyes adjusted to the change from bright sunlight outside the house to the dimness of its interior, and I saw that Robin was actually lying on some kind of back board that was made to tilt the feet above the head; the wings were actually his bathrobe. He was wearing pajamas, thankfully.

"Oh, hi Quinn. One moment, please." He pressed a button that was on a remote control he held in his left hand, there was the whine of an electric motor, and the contraption rotated Robin to a standing position. He bent over, unsnapped the straps around his ankles, and stepped free.

He turned to face me and smiled.

"Sorry about that," he said. "Back problems. The inversion table helps."

He shook my hand and gestured to the living room chairs. We sat.

"Is that the computer?" he said, pointing to the laptop. I handed it to him. He flipped the computer open and turned it on.

I said nothing. Robin was typing furiously on the keyboard. I could see that the usual Windows desktop was nowhere to be seen, and that the screen was black with lots of white text on it, all colons and slashes and arcane words. Robin had bypassed the normal interface and was peering into the parts of the computer unknown to mere mortals such as I.

"There's more than just e-mails on here that are encrypted," he said. He turned the computer toward me, showing me a jumble of text I couldn't hope to understand.

"What is it?" I asked.

He turned the computer back to face him, and shook his head.

"Don't know, exactly," he said. He closed the computer and stood. "Give me a few days and I will, though."

I nodded and stood.

"Call me when you get it cracked," I said,

He was already up and moving toward the back of his house, where he kept one bedroom filled with computers and computer parts—his Lair of Evil Genius, as he called it.

Over his shoulder, not even looking back, he said, "I will. Close the door on your way out."

CHAPTER 14

A couple of hours later Ping and I were running along the side of the road, near the Little Spokane River. It was cold—no more than thirty degrees—and the sky was as gray as the stairs in a military hospital. I was huffing along, sweat running in cold rivulets down my neck. I had a watch cap on my head—now that I kept it shaved down close, my head got cold pretty quick. Hair is greatly underestimated as an insulator.

Ping was into the rhythm of the run, breathing a lot easier than I, but he was also covered in a light sheen of sweat. We had been running for about forty-five minutes now. I had come a long way in a few months time. I was running ten miles a day, plus the weights every other day. Sometimes I brought Powder along, much to Ping's annoyance. Today I had left him at the apartment.

Today would be a boxing day—we planned to get into the ring at Beau Tyler's gym around three in the afternoon. That was a good time to go there. Most people were still at work. The only people at the gym at that time of day were the really serious ones—like us.

"What do you make of it?"

"Make of what?" Ping said.

"Of all those guys at Minor's house last night."

"Still not sure," Ping answered. We slowed down to wait

for a light at the cross street. There was a lady at the bus stop, sitting on the bench. She looked to be around twenty, with a two-year-old girl sitting next to her. The girl's belly button was exposed to the cold, her pink coat too small to cover it. The twenty-year-old lit a cigarette and leaned over to talk to the baby.

As we jogged past, Ping bent over and said, "Why don't you just give the kid her own cigarette lady? It'll be quicker that way."

The woman had no chance to reply, but she craned her neck around and watched as we hoofed it down the street. I'm pretty sure nobody had ever talked to her that way before. I smiled.

A car went by and splashed water on our legs. It was cold.

"Minor's into something," Ping said. "Can't be anything too big."

"Cause he's an idiot," I offered.

"Yeah," Ping said. "Although the idiot outwitted the system once already."

I spat.

"All right, I'll grant you that," I said. "But it was luck on his part mostly. Dumb luck."

"OK," said Ping. "Here's what I'm wondering, though."

We paused our conversation as we jogged past a dirty looking man in dungarees and a long beard, his pants tucked into his boots.

"You're wondering what?" I said.

"Does what he's into have anything to do with him being in your house?"

I had to think that one over. I stopped running. Ping kept going, and when I realized he wasn't going to stop, I sprinted to catch back up with him.

"Why would you say that?"

He didn't answer.

"What makes you think that, Ping?"

He glanced at me and then turned his face back to the road ahead. I didn't mention the laptop; I was nervous about what we might find on it, but I wasn't sure it had anything to do with Minor or his being in our house.

Ping said, "Just a hunch, really."

"A hunch?"

"Yeah. Something to think about."

We were coming into the downtown area, winding our way down Riverside Avenue and into Riverfront Park.

The Park was the legacy of the 1974 World's Fair, a nice bit of landscaping that had turned a grungy series of side tracks and rail stations into a place for family picnics and occasional music festivals. In the summer there were plenty of food vendors, a Ferris wheel, bicycle rentals, and a carousel with real hand-crafted wooden horses. Pure Americana.

At the moment, it was a deserted place, misted in a fine rain. It was also home to one vagrant sitting under a light post, one black Labrador, me, Ping, and the guy in the latte stand outside the carousel building.

It was the guy in the latte stand who had my interest.

I ordered a double-tall latte with vanilla syrup. Ping ordered a hot tea—somewhat more adventurous than his usual order of plain hot water. Either Ping is having a marvelous joke at my expense, or water is frequently consumed this way in China. Plain. Hot.

We took our beverages and sat under the eaves of the carousel building, out of the rain. We sipped and caught our breath for a while.

"Did you sleep last night?" he said.

"Nope."

"You feel OK?"

"Never felt better," I said. The oddest part was that I meant it. I was probably in the best physical shape of my life. My mind felt clear and focused.

"No more of those attacks?"

"None."

He grunted, and drank some tea.

"You miss it?"

"Sleep?"

He nodded.

"No."

"You suppose it'll cause you to burn out quicker?"

"You mean as in 'die?'"

"Yes."

"Don't know. It's possible, I suppose."

The Labrador came sidling up to Ping, who growled at it. The dog dipped its head and ran away.

"Charming," I said.

"Years of practice."

I drained my cup. I do love a good latte.

"When do we do it?" I said.

He looked at his cup, watching steam rise from it and twirl it in a slow circle in his right hand.

"Soon," he said. "But we need to know if there is some connection. If there's a reason why he was in your house, other than random chance. Don't you want to know what it was?"

"Yeah, I guess I do. But how do we find out?"

"What about your friend Ramsey?"

"First, not my friend. Second, doesn't like me. Third, sure as hell won't like you. And fourth, already suspects me of harboring thoughts of vigilantism."

"So you don't think we'll get much help from him, is that what you're saying?"

"My, but you are quick," I said. "You ever think about going on *Jeopardy*?"

"Too many white guys on that show," Ping said, and then he finished his tea.

I went home to let Powder out for a while. He had turned out to be a lot smarter than I would have given him credit for—the first few days I had left him all day long, fully expecting to have a mess to clean up when I got home. But he surprised me by holding his water until I got home. When I saw the little guy scramble for the door those first few days, I felt guilty for leaving him all day. So now we had a routine. We took a walk most mornings to visit Angie's grave, and I made it a point to get home at least twice a day so Powder could get a potty break.

Today, however, when I opened the door he didn't come running to greet me. I walked into the bedroom, figuring he was catching a nap on the bed. He wasn't there.

I walked back to the front door and looked down the steps. No Powder.

I went downstairs and found Mrs. Hudson on the front porch, wringing her hands and looking like she might start crying at any moment. I had a sinking feeling I knew what had happened.

"Mrs. Hudson?" I said.

"Oh, Quinn, I'm so sorry, I didn't think it would happen like that, I thought he would be good."

"Powder?"

Now she did start to cry.

"Yes, yes. I'm so sorry. I let him out, I thought he needed to— and I only turned away for a moment, but then he was gone. I don't know where. I'm so sorry."

I put my arm around her, and she buried her head on my shoulder. I patted her on the back and said, "It's okay, it's okay, we'll find him."

I was not nearly as confident as I sounded, and I was looking over Mrs. Hudson's back, scanning the street, the lawns, and the bushes, looking for any flash of white.

"How long has Powder been gone?"

I gently pushed her away, one hand on each of her shoulders, and looked at her face.

"Do you remember how long?"

I had to find that dog.

He was my last connection to my wife; a living connection to Angie. It was no good telling myself he was "just a dog." Damn.

"I think, maybe a half hour."

She was dabbing a handkerchief at her eyes now.

A half hour. I looked up and down the street again.

"Mrs. Hudson, do you have any idea which way he might have gone?"

She shook her head. Of course not.

I looked at my watch. I didn't have much time, but I could at least make a circuit of the neighborhood.

"Quinn," Mrs. Hudson said. "I'm afraid I've done an unforgivable thing, letting your dog run away."

"Not unforgivable," I said. "Listen, Mrs. Hudson, I need your help."

She sucked in a quick sob, and then nodded her head.

"I need you to stay here on the front porch and watch for Powder. I'm going to go looking for him, but if he comes back I want you to be here. OK?"

She nodded again.

I took off at a slow jog, crossing the street to the Langford place. Sometimes Powder liked to watch the Langford's cat prowling among the azaleas, so I thought that was as good a place as any to start. I circled around behind their house, and surveyed the back yard. Powder was not there. I went back to the street and kept on jogging, peering in between houses and behind hedges. When I had covered about a mile, I turned back and jogged down the other side, repeating the search. No luck.

As I approached Mrs. Hudson's house (my house, I

thought, it's also my house now), I found myself hoping Powder would be on the front porch with her.

No such luck.

"Have you seen him?"

She shook her head and shrugged, so I just kept jogging. I went a mile in the opposite direction from my previous searching and was fairly tired when I got back to the house. Mrs. Hudson had been crying again.

I sat on the big chair on the front porch and laid my head back, breathing heavy and sweating. I had already run ten miles this morning, and had done a pretty good workout with weights too—the extra four miles had taken most of my remaining strength.

Mrs. Hudson said nothing, but she went inside quietly and returned in a few moments with a pitcher and a glass filled with ice on a silver tray. She set these down on the small table between the swing she had been sitting on and the chair I was occupying, and poured me a glass of lemonade. Being a gentleman of exceptional breeding, I picked it up and slurped loudly.

"Thank you," I said.

"It's the least I could do."

She sat on the swing and fidgeted with her sleeve.

I looked at the tray and its matching silver pitcher.

"You are an amazing woman, Mrs. Hudson," I said. "This is the first time anyone has ever served me hand-squeezed lemonade on a silver platter."

I finished my glass of lemonade and set it on the tray next to the pitcher.

Mrs. Hudson laughed.

"What?" I said.

She just shook her head.

"It isn't real, Quinn."

I looked at the pitcher and tray.

"Well, it may not be real silver, but still…"

"No, no, no! The silver is real. I meant the lemonade."

I must have looked puzzled, because she said, "It was Country Time."

I nodded, and looked at my watch. It was after three. I had to get going.

I was very worried about Powder, and even more worried that so much of my emotional self was tied up in that stupid little dog.

Rudyard Kipling may have been right: "Why give your heart to a dog to tear?"

Chapter 15

Ping and I met downtown, outside the Spokane Public Library building. It was a nice architectural mix of traditional stateliness and modern lines. Ping almost sprinted down the wide marble steps from the upper floor down to the street level lobby.

"Good afternoon, my Black friend," Ping said. He was given to temporary episodes during which he thought such puns were funny.

"Afternoon," I said.

We exited the lobby through the beautiful glass doors, which were always covered in fingerprint smudges. The day was bright, sunshine streamed between the tall downtown buildings, creating stark shadows on the streets. It was cold, but I didn't mind and neither did Ping. We walked quickly along the sidewalk, looking like two men on important business.

"What did you find out?" I said.

"Well," Ping said, "Minor owns the house. Or rather he and First Union Bank own it. Makes his payments on time. The man we saw him with, the one who seemed to be in charge, is named Tony Cerazini. He's got a record for minor cons, insurance fraud, stuff like that. I think Danny Minor is working for him—doing grunt work. Maybe setting fires, maybe staging auto accidents, that kind of thing."

I stuffed my hands in my pockets.

"So do you think there's any connection between Angie's death and all of that?" I asked.

Ping shrugged.

"Could have been," he said.

I thought about it.

"Part of Angie's job was finding the frauds among the insurance cases she worked," I said.

Ping nodded. He breathed out and I noticed I could see his breath in the air. Colder than I had thought.

"Could be," Ping said, "Maybe she uncovered one of Cerazini's scams. Or maybe she was about to, and he wanted it stopped. Then maybe he hired Minor to shut her up."

"To kill her, you mean." I could hear the bitterness in my own voice, but that didn't bother me.

"Right," Ping said. "But it could be there's no connection at all."

We walked on in silence for a while.

I began to slow down as I thought about all this, and finally I found a bench. We sat down.

An old black man sat on the corner across the street, right in front of Walgreen's. He was playing an intricate melody on a small white flute. He had a book on his lap, and it was held open with one of those leather straps with weights in both ends, made just for that purpose. Every now and then he paused in his playing and turned the page. Then he began playing again, picking up right where he left off. Somehow he managed to do it in a way that sounded as if the music were meant to pause in just that particular spot. I listened for a while, and watched several people stop briefly to drop a few coins into his cup. Helluva way to make a living, I thought.

"What do you think, Ping?"

"I think he should try to learn some popular tunes instead of all that improvisation," Ping said. "He'd bring in more money."

I tried to look exasperated with Ping, but I'm not sure it came across. He just chuckled.

"What I meant was, what do you think we ought to do about Minor? Or about Cerazini?"

Ping nodded. "Yeah, I thought that's what you meant. But I stand by my critique of the flute guy."

He shuffled his feet across the ground in front of us.

"Quinn, I'm with you on this. Minor is going down, of that I'm sure. But I just don't know about Cerazini. It might be that this is not connected to him in any way, in which case it would be very wrong for us to punish him."

I leaned back against the bench.

"Yeah, but if he did hire Danny Minor to kill Angie…"

"Then we have to take him down, too," Ping said. "Because first of all that makes him responsible—and secondly he probably has already ordered you taken out as well."

I laughed, nervously.

"You thought so too?" I said. "Funny how great minds run on similar tracks."

Ping punched me in the shoulder.

"Only great mind around here I know of is mine," he said.

"How'd you find out all this stuff?" I asked.

"Well, I can't share that with you, Honorable Mister Black," he said. "I have to protect my sources."

"Right," I said.

I thought for a moment, then said, "I may have found something myself."

Ping waited.

"Angie's computer had some encrypted emails on it. I have a guy working on cracking the password."

I stared at the ground.

"Angie and I didn't have secrets from one another. I don't know what this might mean."

Ping put a hand on my shoulder.

"I'm sure Angie wasn't keeping secrets from you, Quinn. But a lot of companies use encryption on their confidential files. Angie worked for insurance lawyers. It's not that much of a surprise that some of her files would have a password on them."

He was trying to stop my mind from going to bad places—to places where Angie had secrets I didn't know about. I appreciated him for it.

We listened to the flute guy for a while before we left, but he never did play anything I recognized.

Ping was right. If the guy would learn some popular tunes he'd make more money.

I took the bus home from downtown. I was riding along thinking of Powder, sort of caught up in that bus-riding daze, when someone sat down beside me. This was odd, since the bus was mostly empty. I looked up from my intense study of the rubber flashing around the edge of the cracked window and I saw that my seatmate was Stan Ramsey.

"Stan," I said.

"Quinn."

He didn't say anything for a while, just sat there and opened a bag of peanuts. He started eating, and paused for a moment to extend the bag to me. I shook my head and turned back to the window. I could see from his reflection in the glass that he just shrugged and kept on eating.

Finally, without looking away from the window, I said, "So?"

He rolled up the top of the peanut bag, as if this were the cue he had been waiting for.

"So," he said. "You and your friend have been doing a little detective work."

I looked at him now. He was smiling. It was pleasant enough. Hard to get too pissed at him. He just seemed so honest and do-gooderish.

"Have we, now?" I said.

"Yes, as you damn well know."

He twisted the peanut bag in his hands.

"You need to back off, Quinn," he said. "You're too close to this emotionally, and what you're doing is only going to lead to trouble. Most likely trouble only for you, but for sure it's big trouble that you don't want."

I didn't respond.

"You're *not* going to succeed, you know," he said.

"Succeed at what?" I answered. I didn't look at him.

"You know what I mean."

"I'm afraid I don't."

I could see out of the corner of my eye that he was still twisting the peanut bag in his hands. Looking at the bag, not at me.

"Quinn, you can't get away with doing this."

"Why is that, detective?" I said.

"Because it's against the law. Because it's murder."

I nodded. "What was it when Angie died?"

Now it was his turn to be silent.

"Where is the justice in that, Stan?"

"I don't know," he said.

"There's no justice in that," I said. "So don't bother yourself about it."

We both sat, swaying with the motion of the bus as it rounded a tight corner.

Stan said, "Quinn, just give it some more time. Just try to wait it out. It will get better—it always does. It'll become more bearable. I don't want to do this. I don't want to watch you, waiting until you screw up and I have to put you in the system."

"The same system that let my wife's killer go free?" I asked.

He sighed.

"Quinn, I'm asking you to stop thinking about this. Stop trying to deliver your own justice. Please."

The bus was stopping. He put a hand on my shoulder and then he stood up.

"Think about what I've said, Quinn. We're watching. You need to walk away from this."

I didn't answer.

"At least sleep on it," he said.

Then he turned and walked off the bus.

As I watched him turn the corner, I shook my head.

It's no use, Stan. There will be no sleeping on it for me.

Like me, justice never sleeps.

Chapter 16

There is something about rain that only a truly depressed person can appreciate. It was four a.m., and a gentle but steady shower was coming down in Spokane. I was sitting on the concrete steps just behind the convention center, wearing a long dark overcoat, watching the rain pelt the surface of the river, flowing by on its way to wherever it was going. It occurred to me that I didn't really know where the Spokane river was going. Was it the Pacific Ocean? Geography was never my strong suit. Aside from the sound of the rain and a distant train whistle, there was silence.

My wife was dead; her killer was free. I was brain-damaged and unable to sleep. And my dog was lost. Most people are so distracted by life's little problems—getting to work on time, paying the bills—that the real substance of life escapes them. Me, I knew this, because I had lost all of the substance from my life.

I reached into my pocket and pulled out a cigarette. I had quit smoking ten years ago, but lately it hadn't seemed important to I continue my smoke-free lifestyle. Ping hated it—he said it would slow me down, and he made me agree that I would smoke no more than one or two a day. Most days I was able to keep the promise.

I lit my cigarette, but otherwise didn't move much. A pair

of ducks went sliding by on the river. It seemed odd—I would have thought they'd be somewhere far south of here by now, with winter coming on. But there they were, looking as happy as they could be. Are ducks happy?

There was a rustling just behind me, and I was somewhat proud that I wasn't startled by it. I turned my head slowly, and saw an old man shuffling toward me. He must have been in the shadows under the eaves of the Opera House, probably hiding from the rain. I nodded, but didn't turn my head away. Old guy or not, it doesn't pay to let vagrants approach from behind in the dark. Vagrant was exactly what he appeared to be; his clothes were old and ill-fitting and covered with mud and stains. He looked as though his last shave had been a week ago, and I noticed his shoes—once a nice set of wingtips—had no laces.

As he got closer, I could see he wasn't as old as I had at first thought. Fifty maybe. Salt and pepper hair, untrimmed beard, mix-and-match clothing from a rescue mission, I guessed. His eyes still had some sparkle in them, and when he smiled I could see his teeth were basically sound—so he hadn't been homeless for very long.

"Hey buddy," he said. "Can you spare a smoke?"

I nodded, and gave him a cigarette from my pocket. He popped it into his mouth, and I lit it for him. He drew on it long and deep—a real smoker, then.

He stood there, to the side and slightly behind me, smoking the cigarette and watching the ducks with me. I decided he wasn't much of a threat, and turned my attention back to the ducks, too.

"Haven't always been like this," he said.

I didn't look up.

"Me either," I said.

"I mean with no home," he said. He must have thought I misunderstood him.

"That's what I meant, too," I said.

He grunted.

"Didn't figure you for homeless."

I took a final drag on my cigarette, and flicked the butt into the water. Probably not ecologically sound, but it seemed that the situation demanded the gesture.

"Goes to show," I said, "you can't always tell."

Now he seemed to be suspicious of *me*. This gave me no small amusement.

"Say," he said, "You ain't some kind of homo, are you?"

"Why, yes, I am." I tried to keep the smile from my face. "Sapiens. How about you?"

"No need to mock me," he said. He appeared genuinely offended.

"You're right," I said. "I apologize."

This seemed to satisfy him, and he nodded.

"I'm not gay," I said. "Just felt like standing by the river tonight."

He smiled now.

"All right," he said. "Got nothing against them, but you have to be careful."

The ducks were almost completely out of sight now.

"My wife died," I said. I was startled to hear it coming out of my mouth—I don't know why I said it.

"Ah," he said, and it sounded like a sigh. "So did mine. That was the start of it, I guess. I lost interest in everything."

He shrugged.

"And here I am," he said.

I looked at him more closely.

"How long ago?" I asked.

"Little over a year, I guess."

"What did you do? Before…"

He nodded, and waved a hand at me, as if to indicate it wasn't necessary for me to complete the question.

"I drove a truck. Made good money. We have two

grandkids."

"I'm sorry," I said. Suddenly I felt guilty for having categorized him as a vagrant. "I had no idea."

He shrugged, and threw *his* cigarette butt into the river.

"You said it, buddy. You never can tell."

He went back into the shadows and lay down in a dark and presumably dry corner.

I walked back to my car, thinking mostly of the guy in the shadows, the guy who had been a truck driver with a wife and grandkids and then became a homeless man who slept outdoors. I wondered how we ever make it through our lives, and then I remembered a line from Hank Williams —"I'll never get out of this world alive."

My steps seemed to echo loud across the street and I began to feel that creeping sensation of hyper-reality which overcame me every now and then. I slowed down and took a deep breath.

I stopped under the streetlight just behind my car. Someone was sitting in the driver's seat. My heart doubled its pace instantly. Where was my gun? I had decided not to carry it until I could get a proper permit—I didn't want to get picked up for carrying a weapon without a permit until I had finished my business with Danny Minor.

Now I stood, heart pounding, staring at my car and wondering who was in it. I couldn't decide what to do—surely who ever it was saw me in the rear-view mirror. But why didn't he move? And why was he in my car that way, in plain sight?

I started walking again, figuring my only advantage was boldness now. I strode right up to the window and banged on it with my fist.

Angie turned her head and looked at me.

I took a step back, feeling suddenly dizzy. My mouth went as dry as cotton. She's dead.

But there she was, smiling at me with a slightly puzzled

look on her face, as if she wondered what on earth was wrong.

A small black spot appeared on the left side of her head, and I watched with sick fascination as first a trickle, and then a veritable fountain of blood streamed from the spot. The blood spattered on the inside of the car window.

I tripped over something as I took step back, and fell backward. I felt my head strike something, and then I passed out.

It seemed that I was floating in darkness for a long time. Chances are it was only a couple of minutes—maybe just a few seconds, even. A voice seemed to come from a long way off.

"Hey, buddy, are you OK?"

I opened my eyes.

Everything was out of focus, but slowly the image of a man's face took shape in front of me. It was the homeless man.

"Buddy?"

I tried to sit up, but stopped for a moment when I felt a stabbing pain in my neck.

"What happened?" I asked.

"You fell over backwards. Looked like you were having a spell. You been drinking?"

I looked at the face of the homeless man, and realized I only thought it exceedingly large because he was cradling my head in his lap.

Now I did sit up, stabbing pain or no.

I rubbed the back of my neck, which hurt like hell.

"How long was I out?"

The homeless man said, "Not long. A minute or two, maybe. But I'll tell you the truth, the way your head hit that post I thought you were gonna be riding out of here in an ambulance."

I shook my head and looked at my car.

There was no blood on the window.

No Angie—or anybody else—in the front seat.

I had been hallucinating.

This had been a banner day, marking both the first time I had ever had a smoke with a homeless guy and my first full-on hallucination.

I could hardly wait to find out what came next.

I got in my car and drove home.

Chapter 17

"So, you saw your wife?"

Dr. Bibbs was fiddling with a button on his shirt.

"Yes," I said.

Bibb's frowned.

"This wasn't something you could have dreamed? I mean, you're sure you were awake when you saw it?"

"Yeah, I'm sure I was awake."

He nodded.

"Well, Quinn, I can't be sure, but it makes sense. Your body has been going without REM sleep, but somehow you seem to have adapted. It's not unreasonable to think some dream imagery might start creeping into your waking life."

I snorted. "A waking life is the only kind I have, Doc."

"Yes, yes. I know. Now listen Quinn, did you, when you saw this apparition—did you have any kind of a feeling of unreality? Any indication that your state or your perceptions had in any way changed?"

I thought about this for a moment.

"Yeah, maybe. I felt that things had become somehow thin, or translucent. And yet everything seemed hyper-real. But the sensation seemed to pass."

Dr. Bibbs was making notes in a file. When he finished, he laid the file and his pen on the desk. His office hadn't changed at all since the last time I was in it.

"Quinn, I think you may be experiencing some kind of compensating mechanism at work here."

I said nothing.

"You haven't been getting REM sleep—what most of us experience as dreaming. So your mind is compensating by dreaming even in the waking state."

"What can I do about it?" I said.

"I don't know that there is anything you can do about it," he said. "I certainly don't have any real precedent to go on."

He pursed his lips and appeared to be in deep thought. I'm almost certain this is something he had rehearsed, waiting for just such a moment, so he could trot out his act. Something seemed to occur to him.

"You might try lying down and resting," he said.

I laughed.

"I know you can't sleep, Quinn, but hear me out. Perhaps if you relax for a short period each night, even for an hour or so, your brain can get some rest. Re-group, as it were."

"If I'm not sleeping," I said, "What difference will it make?"

He picked up the pen from his desk and twirled it in the fingers of his right hand.

Finally, he said, "Maybe none, to be honest. But there are many studies that show people who meditate, for instance, enter into what's called an 'alpha state.' This is a particular state that is more relaxed, more unfocused, than our normal waking consciousness. You can see the state on an EEG— brainwaves change, flatten out more than usual."

He had my interest.

"Go on," I said.

"Well, Quinn, this alpha state is not the same as REM sleep—it's not as deep in as the delta wave stage, which is what normal sleep looks like—but it is much closer to REM sleep than normal waking consciousness. It's possible that if you could get into alpha for a couple of hours a day, you might get some of the restorative benefits of regular sleep."

I sat back in my chair, and let out a long slow breath. I hadn't even realized I was holding it until that moment.

"Do you think this might reduce these episodes I've been having?"

He dropped the pen into the cup on his desk with all the other pens. Most of them had the name of some drug or other printed on them. The one he had been fidgeting with said PAXIL down the length of the pen. It's quite possible that the only reason Dr. Bibbs agreed to meet pharmaceutical salesmen was for the free pens.

"Maybe," he said. "It might give your brain enough down time that these episodes wouldn't be necessary. Can't guarantee it, but there's a chance."

We were both silent for a while. I was thinking this idea might give me a new lease on life—or at least on sanity. Bibbs was probably thinking about the next paper he would write about me.

"We don't even know exactly how REM sleep works, Quinn," he said. "We just know it is necessary for normal human functioning. Maybe it helps us 'de-fragment' our minds from the previous day's activity. Maybe it's just what happens when the brain is in deep rest. Nobody knows."

"Since you can't get actual REM sleep, it's possible that the next closest thing to it would help," he added. "That next closest thing would be alpha state, or deep relaxation. You've already adapted better than I would have hoped. Perhaps you can adapt further."

I said, "Any suggestions about how I can get to this state you're talking about?"

He nodded, and then reached around to the credenza behind him and retrieved a book. He handed the book to me.

"You might try reading this. It's by a Dr. Nathan Baden, and it's about relaxation techniques. There's an exercise in the second chapter I'd like you to try, a self-hypnosis exercise."

I turned the book over in my hands. It was thin, probably no more than a hundred and fifty pages. The picture of Dr. Baden on the back was about what you would expect—skinny, wearing thick glasses, curly hair and a beard. Probably hadn't been on a date since junior high.

"I'd suggest," Dr. Bibbs said, "that you try the exercise late at night. Even though you're not sleeping these days, that is the time of day your body is accustomed to sleep—from before the accident."

"No," I said.

He looked surprised.

"What?"

"It was not an accident—it was a shooting," I contested. "Mr. Minor hit exactly where he was aiming."

Dr. Bibbs seemed almost annoyed by my poor taste in correcting him.

I stood up.

"Sorry, Doc," I said. "Didn't mean to offend you. But there are some things that need to be stated with accuracy—and that's one of them."

He stood up, too, and seemed to be a relieved that our appointment was almost over.

"Well, of course, Quinn, whatever you say. Just set up your next appointment with Rachel."

I gave him a little salute, exited his office door, and sailed right past Rachel on my way out.

She didn't even look up from her filing as I left.

Chapter 18

At two a.m. I was lying on the sofa in my apartment, practicing my breathing and mentally counting backwards from a hundred. Nothing seemed to change much—I wasn't falling asleep, but I was already used to that. I also wasn't really feeling any other difference, either. I'm not sure what I was expecting—some kind of deep trance, maybe, or an out-of-body experience. None of this was forthcoming.

I let my mind wander.

Physically I had come a very long way in the last few months. I was as fit as I had ever been in my life—running ten miles a day, my body hard and muscular as it had never been before. My scars were mostly healed up—at least they didn't have that angry red look, and they weren't sensitive to the touch anymore.

Ping and I continued to work every day on fighting technique, and shooting at the range. I was getting good—very good—with my Glock. I couldn't put six shots in the same hole like Ping could, but I could cluster them within a one-inch radius. Ping assured me that this was pretty good, and from the little I could remember from my training in boot camp, I knew he was right.

I was ready.

I had somehow managed to mute the grief and rage I felt

when I thought about Angie—it wasn't gone, but it lay just below the surface. A storm beneath a calm sea. Waves rolling across the ocean floor while the surface of the water remained smooth and undisturbed? Was there such a thing?

I wondered where Powder might be. I missed that little dog. I desperately hoped he was all right. Somehow I would have to find him. I had looked around the neighborhood, I had called the pound, and everyday I watched the paper for a "Found Dog" notice.

Tomorrow I would post some fliers offering a reward for his return. Mrs. Hudson would be happy to put some of them up—she was completely guilt-stricken and convinced that his being lost was her fault. I tried to tell her that Powder might have run off from anyone, including me, but she would have none of it.

Of course, I was at least a little angry with her, because in the back of my mind I felt that it was her fault. I would never tell her this.

There was a ringing bell.

I sat up.

I looked at the digital egg timer on the coffee table. An hour had passed.

I shut the beeping timer off, and got up.

Interesting.

I had not gone to sleep—I could at all times hear Mrs. Hudson's snoring, and the sounds of the college kids across the street blundering into their front door after a night of revelry.

No, I had not been sleeping.

But I felt strangely refreshed.

I went to the bathroom and looked in the mirror.

For the first time since being shot, I saw my own smile.

I went back to the kitchenette and put on some water for tea, and sat down at the small table.

So, I had discovered a potential way to replace the function of sleep without actually sleeping. Maybe.

All I had to do was lie down, breath deep and hang out for an hour or so.

I would still be a freak of nature, but a functioning freak. Maybe.

The teakettle began to whistle.

Chapter 19

Brandy slogged water from her bowl on the front porch, her massive tongue operating as if it were a separate entity from her jaw. Ping watched in amusement, slumping back in his chair, his gray sweatshirt soaked with perspiration around the neck and armpits.

I slumped in the other chair.

"Not bad for an old sick guy, huh?" I said.

Ping squinted at me from one eye.

We had just finished a fifteen-mile run.

"Explain to me again," I said between deep breaths, "how we need to push ourselves, not be happy with the status quo, and that we always need to be adding one more mile?"

He gave me a definitive gesture involving only one finger if his right hand, and then lay back in his chair, trying to recover his breath.

Brandy apparently had her fill of water. She sauntered over to Ping, sunk into a heap at his feet, and heaved a deep sigh.

We listened to our own breathing for a while, eventually quieting as our lungs recovered from the run.

It was a crisp November afternoon, but not too cold. The trees had begun to turn, and the maple in front of Ping's house wore a brilliant yellow bouquet of leaves. I found myself wondering if he would bother raking them, or would just let them lie on the ground. My bet was they would lie on the ground.

In the distance, a train blew its whistle.

"Ping, I think it's time we did this thing."

I waited, expecting an argument.

Finally, he said, "I think you're right."

I didn't move, not wanting to show my excitement. I could have done this without him, perhaps, now that I was in top form. But he wouldn't have allowed it.

"But," he said. "What about Cerazini?"

I sighed.

"We don't have any proof so far that he had anything to do with Angie's death," I said. At least until Robin decrypts those e-mails, I thought.

"True. But we know he probably did."

"Ping, I don't think I can kill a man because he probably did."

He nodded.

"If we're right, and he was directly responsible, when we take Minor down Cerazini is going to come straight at you."

I said nothing.

Ping stood up and began pacing back and forth on the porch. Brandy's eyes sprang open and her ears perked up—I turned my head to follow her gaze, and saw a squirrel making its way up the trunk of the maple. Brandy's back twitched, but then she closed her eyes and sighed again. Probably decided the squirrel was already beyond her reach.

Ping said, "We need to flush him out."

"The squirrel?" I said. Ping looked annoyed. He thought I was making some kind of bad joke.

"No," Ping said. "Cerazini. We need to know if he was behind it."

"And how do we find that out?" I asked. "Just call and ask?"

Ping stopped pacing.

"Yes."

I stared at him.

"What?" was all I could manage.

"Not quite that simple, of course, but close to it."

Ping went inside the house. Brandy got up and walked over to my chair. She leaned her body up against my leg, and I obliged her by scratching her back.

I heard Ping inside rummaging around; then there was silence. For a brief moment I thought I heard him talking to someone.

He came back out to the porch and tossed me an Alaskan Amber Ale. He sat down and twisted the lid from his own.

He had the cordless phone tucked into the pocket of his sweats.

"Did you call him?" I asked. I couldn't believe he had actually called Cerazini.

Ping smiled.

"Yeah, but he wasn't home. I left a message."

He took a big slug of beer, and smiled at me.

I shook my head and took a drink of my own beer.

We decided hanging out at Ping's place was not the best idea, since it would have been easy for Cerazini to trace the call back. In these days of "star sixty-nine," this wasn't the complex operation it had once been. So we drove back into the city and over to St. Vincent's. Father O'Dell had invited me to be part of his weekly poker game, and it seemed as good a place as any to hide out for a while. And I admit it—I kind of liked the guy.

We pulled into a parking spot behind the church and got out. A priest stood by the back door smoking a cigarette. I didn't recognize him. He was younger than O'Dell, with blond hair and a nose that made him resemble a hawk.

"Now there's something you don't see every day," Ping

said.

I walked over and held out my hand to the priest.

"I'm Quinn Black," I said. "You must be Father Westcott."

He smiled, nodded, and shook my hand, keeping the cigarette between his teeth.

"This is my friend Ping." I said and gestured to my left.

Father Westcott took the cigarette from his mouth and stomped it under his left foot.

"Just Ping?" he said.

"Just," Ping answered.

Father Westcott bent down and picked up the cigarette butt from under his shoe, and held it out apologetically before tossing it into metal trash bin behind him.

He shrugged.

"Sorry you had to see that," he said. "It's practically my only vice."

Ping must have looked skeptical.

"No, really," Westcott said. "And I know I shouldn't do it, but it's hard to give it up. I started when I was in the Navy."

I realized why I had liked him so quickly.

"Where did you serve?" I asked.

"The Gulf," he said.

Ping slapped Westcott on the back, and said, "OK, Squid, we gonna play some cards or not?"

Westcott looked slightly taken back by Ping.

"Squid?" Westcott said.

I winked at him.

"We're Marines," I said.

Westcott smiled, and opened the back door of the church, motioning us to go in first.

"That explains it," he said. "Jarheads."

Yep, I liked him.

I never would have thought St. Vincent's was a good place

to play cards, but it was. Father O'Dell had an office in the basement he had outfitted just for the purpose—including a real card table complete with green felt and drink holders, a small refrigerator, and a credenza that doubled as a bar.

We sat around the table, and O'Dell laid out the cards and chips, while Westcott went about the business of pouring the drinks.

"What would you like, Mr. Black?" Westcott said.

Westcott took the bottles from under the credenza and set them up on top of it, along with the glasses. He took the ice from the fridge and set it on the credenza too.

"Got any scotch?" I said.

He nodded. "You bet. Neat?"

"Yeah. And please call me Quinn." I was beginning to see way too much irony in being called "Mr. Black," especially by a priest.

Ping said he would have the same. Westcott and O'Dell opted for the bourbon. We sat down and played cards. I have always been a fan of your more standard draw poker, but Ping was determined to play something called "Guts," and since he was dealing that's what we did. I'm still not sure I understand the rules of this particular version of the game, which probably explains why I lost fifty-seven dollars.

I was down about twenty bucks when Westcott said, "So, what about you boys? Where'd you do your time?"

I looked at him for a moment and realized he wasn't all that different from Ping and me—he was in his mid-to-late thirties, relatively fit, and not the stereotype of a service veteran.

"We were in the Gulf too," I said. Ping said nothing—he was looking at his cards and I'm sure he had decided that this was a ruse designed to upset the game somehow. Ping is paranoid like that.

"I have to ask," I said. "You're both vets, and you're both priests, and yet, here we are, drinking liquor and playing cards in the basement of your church. Isn't that a little irregular?"

O'Dell shrugged, and when he did his collar gapped large—he had loosened it before we started playing.

"We're both vets, and we're both priests," he said, as if this was a complete answer. "You playing?"

I played. Or gave a good impersonation of playing, anyway.

After a couple more hands, O'Dell said, "Father Westcott and I met when we were stateside after the Gulf. We found that we had similar views on certain issues." He took long drink of bourbon and grimaced. "And so we managed to end up taking this church together."

"You can do that?" Ping asked.

Westcott nodded. "Much like any other political organization, there are ways to get what you want within the Church."

The sound of shattering glass ended our witty repartee. We all looked at one another.

Ping said, "Were you expecting any deliveries through the windows tonight?"

"No," O'Dell said.

We all got up and headed down the hallway to the stairs. We all took them two at a time. O'Dell grabbed a baseball bat on his way up the stairs without even looking down for it—he must have put it there for the purpose, and he had done so recently enough that he knew exactly where it was. I eyed the bat.

"What about turning the other cheek?" I asked as we made our way up the stairs.

Father O'Dell smiled and said, "Oh, I'd never actually hit anyone with it. But they don't know that, do they?"

I shrugged and tried to decide whether I believed him.

When we got upstairs we found shards of multicolored glass sprayed across the floor of the narthex. Lying in the midst of the glass was a concrete block, and tied to the block was a note. Of course.

Whoever had thrown the block had tossed it through one of the small side windows in the narthex, so at least they hadn't ruined any of the antique stained glass in the sanctuary—but I had the feeling that replacing the narthex glass wouldn't exactly be cheap, either.

O'Dell opened the front door a crack and peered out for a moment, and then opened it all the way and stepped out onto the front steps. Westcott was using a small pocketknife to cut the note loose from the block. He unfolded it, glanced at it, and handed it to Ping.

"It's for you," Westcott said.

Ping looked the note over and then passed it on to me.

"Well, Honorable Quinn, this makes things more interesting," he said.

I read the note.

"To the Jap guy and Quinn Black—We know what you're doing. Stop sneaking around me and my business, and stay out of my way, or you'll end up like your wife. Back off."

O'Dell came back in.

"Whoever it was, they're gone," he said.

I handed the note to O'Dell—since Ping and I were responsible for the broken glass, I figured he deserved to at least read the note.

"Eloquent," O'Dell said, and handed the note back to me.

"I wish they could get the nationality right," Ping said.

"They?" Westcott said.

"Yeah, they," I said. "It's one guy, mainly, but I'm sure he was accompanied tonight by his henchmen."

Ping's eyebrows went up. "I can't believe you just used the word 'henchmen' in a sentence," he said.

Father O'Dell locked the front door, and motioned with his Louisville Slugger toward the back of the sanctuary.

"Why don't we go downstairs, gentlemen," he said. "We can call this in to Spokane's finest, and that will give me the documentation I need for the insurance company. And then you can tell me what this is all about."

We sat in the church's kitchen, drinking coffee now instead of scotch. Ping drank his usual hot water, only for some reason he decided to splurge and had a lemon wedge too. Ping watched me carefully—waiting to see how much I was going to tell Fathers Westcott and O'Dell.

O'Dell sipped his coffee, and said, "Well?"

"It's the man who killed my wife," I said.

"Someone killed your wife?" Westcott looked from me to Father O'Dell, waiting for an answer.

"Yeah," I said.

"We've been watching him," Ping offered. It was not lost on me that Ping was sticking to what was in the note. Nothing ventured, there, since that was going to be a matter of record as soon as the police arrived.

"I don't understand," Westcott said. "If he killed your wife, why isn't he in jail?"

I sat my coffee cup down.

"Good question," I offered. "One I ask myself at least ten times a day."

This didn't appear to satisfy Father Westcott. Father O'Dell just remained quiet, probably knowing I was about to tell them more.

"He got off on a technicality," I said. "Not enough evidence to convict him. So he's free."

"We've been hoping to catch him at something else," Ping said. "Thought maybe we could still get him sent to jail."

"Apparently he's smarter than you thought," Father O'Dell said.

"Apparently," I answered. "Look, I'm sorry about your

window. I'd be happy to pay for it."

O'Dell laughed. "Not if you knew how old it was."

I opened my mouth, but he waved me off.

"No, no, don't worry about that. That's why we have insurance. I do wonder, though, why did this person wait until you were in here? Why throw their rock through the church's window instead of through yours?"

Ping said, "Probably just following us. Saw us go in here. Thought this would be a good way to send their message."

I nodded.

"Ping's right," I said. "Most likely they just wanted to show us how tough they are. Not afraid of anything, including God."

Through the tiny window above us—it was one of those little basement windows that serve little purpose beyond letting in a little light and collecting leaves and cigarette butts—there was the flashing blue light from a police cruiser.

"Shall we go up and tell our story?" said Father O'Dell.

Somehow the way he said it made it clear he knew there was more than we were telling.

I looked at Ping, who just shrugged.

We went upstairs, and were greeted by two uniformed officers.

"Good evening officers," said Father O'Dell.

"Evening, Father," said one of the men. He appeared to be slightly older than the other officer. He looked at Ping and me. "What happened here?"

Before I could say anything, Father O'Dell said, "Vandals, I suppose. They threw a concrete block through one of the narthex windows."

We all walked around to the side of the building so we could see the damage. I was curious about where Father O'Dell was taking this.

The lead officer wrote something on a notepad while his

partner looked around at the ground under the window.

"Any idea who might have done this?" the younger officer asked.

"I can't think of anyone I know who would do this," O'Dell said, and he shot Ping and me a look. Say nothing. "I'm afraid I don't have much more to tell you. I really just needed to file a report for insurance purposes."

The older man looked at Ping and me, and then at Father Westcott. Westcott was studying O'Dell closely.

"What about you, Father? You have anything to add?" the older cop looked at Westcott.

"No, I have nothing to add," he said. "We didn't really see anything. We were all in the basement, and just heard the glass break. When we came up, we found the block."

The older cop wrote something else on his notepad.

"OK, let me get my stuff from the cruiser. I'll need you to fill out a statement. We can do that here. I'll leave you a copy for your insurance guy."

Ping looked at me, and I shrugged. Of course, that I had no idea what was going on.

I had my hands in my pockets, and my right hand was wrapped around the note.

Chapter 20

We sat around the card table again, but without the benefit of cards.

"Why did you do that?" I asked Father O'Dell.

He let out a long sigh and shook his head.

"Because I felt we had told them all they needed to know," he said. He looked at me. "I'm not sure you've told me all I need to know, but I can guess part of it."

Father Westcott was watching O'Dell closely.

"Father, this may have been a great mistake," Westcott said.

O'Dell nodded his head. "It may," he said.

"Listen," I said. "Thank you for what you did. The last thing I want is more time spent with the police."

Westcott raised an eyebrow.

"After Angie was killed," I said, choosing my words with care, "I went through so many statements, lineups, and court dates. We had the guy—he was in jail—but because someone failed to get the right warrants, conduct the searches in the right way, Danny Minor walked."

I took a deep breath. All true up until now.

"I have done what I could to find another way that the police could arrest him. Every road has been a dead end."

Ping watched me very closely now, and I know he was

wondering if I was going to blow it now by telling the whole truth. Sometimes a guy just can't get any credit.

"So," I said, "I have had about all the time in police stations I want. Since Minor didn't sign the note, there's no way to prove he was behind it. So once again I would be hauling him in there just to watch the police let him go. Thanks, but no thanks."

Father O'Dell ran the fingers of his right hand along the inside of his loosened collar.

"You see, Father Westcott, we have decided correctly," he said after a moment. Something in his voice made it sound as if he might believe otherwise.

"I'm not so sure," Westcott said. "But the decision is made. Time will tell."

He busied himself cleaning up the drink glasses and cards on the table.

Ping stood up.

"We should go," he said.

I shook hands with Father O'Dell, and the look he gave me was an admonishment: Don't do anything unwise.

I fully intended to avoid such a thing.

Ping and I rode in his truck, and I watched the church getting smaller in the passenger side mirror. The message printed across the bottom of the mirror seemed funny to me: right below the image of the shrinking church were the words OBJECTS IN MIRROR MAY BE CLOSER THAN THEY APPEAR.

We crossed the river, and Ping made a left onto Riverside Drive. We circled around and headed back north on Division.

"Where are we going?" I asked.

"I think you know," he said.

I did.

I withdrew my Glock from the glove box where I had left

it earlier when we entered the church, and checked to make sure the clip was full and secure. It was.

Ping eased the car into a space on the street. I looked up at the street sign. Alba Avenue—that put us about four blocks over from Minor's house in Peaceful Valley.

We got out of the truck and closed the doors quietly. I looked at my watch. It was just before two a.m. The neighborhood was mostly quiet, although there seemed to be a party going on at a house just down the street. A couple of men stood on the front porch, leaning on each other and both laughing. I'd say one of them had just told a joke. No doubt it seemed funnier if you were drunk.

I looked at Ping across the hood of the truck.

"We go straight in," he said. "They won't be expecting us so soon, so we have surprise on our side. We'll come from the back, though. They won't see us until it's too late."

I hefted the Glock, and released the safety.

"Let's go," I said. I was surprised at how solid my voice sounded.

We started walking. We had spent enough time in the neighborhood over the last few weeks that we knew all we had to do was walk straight through the yard of the house we were parked in front of, across their backyard, and repeat the process two more times. That would bring us right through Minor's back yard.

It was dark, but not too dark—the moon was out and nearly three quarters full. I kept my eyes open for dogs and unsuspecting people in their own backyards. We saw neither, although we did startle a cat that was rooting in a garbage can. It screeched and fled across a fence, knocking the lid from the garbage can to the ground.

Ping and I froze, waiting to see if anyone would come to investigate the noise, but there was no sign anyone had heard, so we continued.

Soon enough we were looking at the back of Minor's house. We stood under some low trees, hidden in shadow. A light was on upstairs, but the curtain was drawn and we couldn't see anyone through the window. No one was on the back porch.

I looked at Ping and he nodded. We sprinted across the backyard, up the driveway beside the house, and rounded the corner on the front porch with—our guns drawn and ready. Ping leapt up the front step and onto the porch. It was concrete, so there was no creaking noise. I followed.

We looked into the tiny window on the front door, but there was no light on in the living room. Ping tried the doorknob—it turned easily in his hand. He pushed it inward, and there was only a slight squeak. I made a mental note that the next time we did something like this we should bring a can of WD-40.

We stepped softly into the living room. Angry voices came down the stairwell from an upstairs room.

"I'm telling you he won't be anymore trouble," one voice said. I recognized it immediately—Danny Minor.

"You don't know that," another voice said. This one I didn't recognize. "Who'd have thought he would be so interested after he got shot in the head? That didn't scare him off, did it?"

I took a step toward the stairs. My foot kicked against something. It must have been a piece of furniture, because it made a loud scraping noise.

The next thing I knew, pain exploded across my back and I hit the floor hard. I rolled over and looked up, making out the shadow of a man holding a baseball bat.

"We got company!" someone shouted. It was another man—not the one who had hit me. I couldn't see Ping, but I could see that the man standing over me was raising his weapon for another swing.

I scooted forward and swept my legs behind his feet. He landed with a crash on what sounded like a glass table.

There was another scuffle in the room, but I couldn't see it. I assumed that's where Ping was, and I scrambled to my knees. The lights came on.

Danny Minor was standing at the foot of the stairs with one hand on the light switch and the other holding a gun. He surveyed the room, and when he saw me he smiled. He raised his gun in my direction.

I fired my Glock, and he spun around and fell face forward on the stairs.

"Quinn!"

I turned to see Ping in the corner of the room, blood trickling from his left eye. A man stood over him, pointing a gun straight at his head. I raised my gun to shoot him, but before I could he crouched and turned to face me. He had seen my reflection in the window behind Ping.

Ping took the opportunity to grab the base of a large wooden lamp on the table next to his head, and threw it at the man's back. The man's head snapped forward and landed face down on the floor, writhing in pain.

I ran to Ping and helped him up. Except for the cut above his eye he seemed fine. He found his gun on the floor and tucked it into his coat.

We both turned our attention to Minor, who had slowly leveraging himself up from the floor. His blood-soaked left hand hung limply at his side. I had apparently hit him in the elbow. Ping grabbed me and pulled me across the room to the back door, and the next thing I knew we were in the backyard.

Before I could ask what he was doing, I saw the flashing play of blue lights across the trees. Police had arrived out front, and Ping had gotten us out of the house just in time. He must have seen them coming through one of the front windows.

We ran through the darkened yards again, only a lot faster

this time.

As we made our way into the last yard, a man came onto the porch in his underwear. He opened his mouth, as if he were going to shout at us, but Ping waved his gun and the man quickly ran back inside the house.

We climbed into the truck and sat for a moment. Ping looked up and down the street. He saw no one, so he started the truck and calmly drove us out of the neighborhood.

When we got back to Ping's place, I showered first while he kept a watch from the front porch, then we switched.

I was sitting on the porch, peering out at the darkness, when Ping came out with coffee for us both. He sat down.

"How's the eye?" I said.

"It's fine. I won't need any stitches."

We sat for a little while and sipped our coffees.

"What went wrong?" I asked finally.

"They were waiting for us," he said. "Or probably it's more accurate to say they were waiting for someone. Probably didn't expect it to be us."

"Yeah," I said. "I think you're right about that."

Brandy padded out onto the porch and lay down between us. She was asleep in seconds.

"Now what?" I said.

Ping finished his coffee.

"We need to get some rest," he said. "Then we decide what to do. One of us needs to stay on watch."

I smiled, even though I knew he couldn't see it. He wouldn't have gotten the joke anyway.

"I'll stand watch first," I said. "You go sleep."

He didn't argue, just took his cup and went inside. Brandy grunted, then got up and followed him. I think that was the dog way of saying *make up your mind.*

I sat in the dark and watched, wide awake.

A few minutes after dawn, Ping came out onto the porch. He did it silently, and I think in part he was trying to sneak around me to see if I had fallen asleep on watch.

"You stay out here all night?" he said.

I nodded.

"You fall asleep?"

I shook my head.

"Humph." He scratched his head, still looking at me.

"Still got insomnia?"

"Probably the worst case ever," I said. I got up from the chair. "Let's have some breakfast."

We went inside and Ping made the coffee. I found eggs, bacon, and tomatoes in the fridge. I fried the bacon first, then used the grease to fry the eggs until they were just a touch crispy. I served this onto plates, and then sliced the cold tomato and divvied up the slices between me and Ping.

I also gave Brandy a slice. She's the only dog I ever met who liked tomato. I wondered if Powder might like tomato, and I wondered where he was at that moment. If he was lost forever? I couldn't think about it. I turned my attention back to the food.

We ate without talking, and cleaned up the mess.

Then we sat in the living room, where we both had a good view out the front window and could keep an eye on the driveway.

"Well?" I said.

Ping let out a sigh. "Well, he knows what we want now. And he knows we're serious."

"That would seem reasonable to assume," I said.

Ping said, "What we don't know is what happened with the cops, how bad was Minor hurt, and where is he now?"

I was watching a police cruiser pull up in front of the house, but since Ping was looking at me, he hadn't seen it yet.

"We may be about to find out all those things," I said, and pointed out the window.

Ping looked and said, "Oh. Shit."

"I couldn't have said it better myself," I answered.

Brandy, who had been curled up on the rug, raised her head, looked out the window, and then went back to sleep. Good thing we hadn't left her on watch.

Stan Ramsey got out of the car and walked up to the front porch. He knocked politely. Ping doesn't have a doorbell.

I opened the door.

"Ramsey," I said.

"Quinn," he said.

He stepped inside without waiting to be invited. His eyes scanned up and down the hall, relaxing when he saw Ping leaning against the kitchen doorway.

"Do come in," Ping said.

I walked around Ramsey and went to the coffeepot. I warmed up my cup.

"Coffee, Ramsey?"

"Sure."

He was looking at Ping's eye.

"That hurt much?" he asked Ping.

I handed Ramsey his coffee, and leaned back against the kitchen counter, sipping my own.

Ping said, "Not too much."

Ramsey grunted.

"You men want to talk to me about last night?" he asked after a while.

"What about it?" I said.

"About how you broke into Danny Minor's place and tried to kill him."

"Ah, that," I said. "What makes you think that was us?"

"Just a wild guess," Ramsey answered.

Interesting, I thought. If Ramsey was telling the truth it meant Minor hadn't given us up—which meant Minor was definitely planning to kill us. Always good to know where you stand.

"Someone tried to kill Danny Minor?" Ping said.

Ramsey took a drink of coffee and grimaced. It wasn't bad coffee, so I assumed he must of burned his tongue.

"Look, guys," he said. "If this is how you want to play it, that's fine by me. But you're going to get yourselves killed. I can't help you if you keep messing around with Danny Minor. Maybe you'll end up getting innocent people killed, too. Not everyone who lives on that street is a hardened criminal, you know."

I honestly hadn't thought about that. It would have been easy to accidentally shoot one of the neighbors through a window.

"So let me tell you how it's going to go," Ramsey said. "We're going to be watching you very closely. The next time you try to pull something like this, we're going to arrest you."

"Fair enough," I said.

Ramsey stepped closer to me, and poked me in the chest with his finger.

"You don't know what you're messing with here, Quinn," he said. "If Minor knows it was you who tried to kill him last night—and my guess is he does know—he'll be looking for you. Looking to kill you."

He turned and looked at Ping now.

"Getting arrested by me could be the least of your worries."

Ping said nothing.

Ramsey threw up his hands and walked toward the door.

"Ramsey, are you actually worried about us?" I said.

He stopped in the doorway.

"When you serve me coffee that bad?" he said. "Not very

likely."

We watched him get in his car and drive away.

"He's worried about us," I said to Ping.

"So am I," Ping said.

Brandy grunted.

Chapter 21

I needed to clear my head, so I drove back to my apartment. I decided that while I was clearing my head I might also work on finding my dog, so I stopped at Kinko's on the way home and had fifty signs printed up, offering a reward for Powder's return.

I went in the side door to the house and climbed the stairs to my apartment. There was a note stuck to the door, written on a small piece of stationery with a bluebird printed in the top right hand corner. It was a colorful, realistic bluebird, and reminded me of the artwork you see in those pamphlets the Mormons and Jehovah's Witnesses hand out. Too real, too perfect.

The note said:

"Quinn, Please come and see me when you get home. Mrs. Hudson"

I smiled and unlocked the door, went into the apartment, and lay the note and my reward signs on the side table by the door. I went to the fridge, opened an Alaskan Amber Ale, and plopped onto the couch. I thought about turning on the television, but couldn't imagine there would be anything on except the usual mindless drivel, so I decided to leave it off.

I sat quietly and drank my beer. It occurred to me that it was still not yet noon and that drinking a beer before noon might be considered bad behavior by some people. Especially if the beer drinker were someone who had just lost their wife, who's medical leave was going to run out very soon, and who had less than ten thousand dollars in the bank.

I winced.

Money wasn't something I had given a lot of thought to lately, but thoughts of my negative cash flow were looming large. I picked up the phone book on the table by the couch and looked up a number. I dialed.

"Averson Insurance Agency, how may I direct your call?" a too-pleasant voice answered.

"This is Quinn Black. I need to speak to Wade, please."

"Just a moment," the woman's voice said, and I was treated to an earful of a dreadful song from the fifties. Something about someone's girlfriend struck by a train in his 409, all set to surfing music.

After a moment, the music stopped and Wade Averson answered, "Quinn, how are you?"

His voice had what I had come to think of as "that tone"—the one people use when they think they need to sound concerned about my welfare. It borders on baby-talk. I despise that tone.

"Fine, Wade. As good as can be expected when my wife is dead." Yes, I admit that I said it deliberately for the shock value. Angie would have approved.

He was silent for a moment, but quickly regained his composure.

"I've been expecting your call, Quinn."

It was a good thing I had called him instead of stopping by his office. Wade had called me only days after I regained consciousness, wanting to settle up Angie's life insurance policy. I had become very angry, and told him I would call him when I was good and goddamned ready. Or something similar to that, anyway.

His manner now—and "I've been expecting your call"—said that he was gloating just a little. It said you-all-call-when-the-money-runs-out. It pissed me off.

"Just get me my money, Wade. You can talk to my attorney and get the papers you need."

I hung up.

I was not what you might call well-adjusted yet.

I sighed and finished the beer. So much for the money problem. When the insurance check finally came, I would be Spokane's newest millionaire. As the great philosopher Forrest Gump said, "that's one less thing."

If only my best friend were still around so I could share it with her.

Mrs. Hudson was in her living room—or the "parlor," as she liked to call it—drinking tea. She smiled when I came in, but I noticed she didn't get up. She looked a little pale. I went over and sat down next to her, laying my hammer, tacks, and reward signs on the end table.

"You made signs?" she asked.

"Yes, ma'am, I did."

"Good. I feel just terrible, Quinn, I really do."

I put up a hand to stop her.

"Mrs. Hudson, I really won't hear any more about it. It was not your fault that Powder ran off. He's a dog. Dogs do such things."

She nodded and grew silent. I noticed she was glancing over my shoulder, and I turned to see what she was looking at. It was a portrait of her late husband, Henry. The photograph looked as if had been taken in the forties or early fifties, perhaps. Dr. Hudson was wearing an impeccable three-piece suit, and his hair was slicked back. He was an imposing man. My guess is his bedside manner probably left a little to be desired, but that was probably true of most physicians of that time. Those were the days when doctors were almost a law unto themselves. Dr. Hudson's face seemed to radiate that ideal—that he was a law unto himself.

"Bad day?" I asked.

"Yes, I suppose it is," she said.

I turned back to face her.

"Missing your husband?"

"Yes," she said. She pointed to the coffee table, and I noticed she had tea settings for two.

"I was hoping you would join me for tea," she said. I pretended not to know that the second setting had not been for me.

"I would be delighted," I said. She poured me tea, and I dropped a couple of sugars in the cup. The tea was quite good.

"Are you going to put up the signs this afternoon?" she asked.

"Yes, as soon as we finish our tea," I said.

"Do you think it will work?"

I frowned. "I hope so. It's been over a week now, but I think it's likely that someone found Powder and just took him in."

She smiled.

"He is quite an adorable little fellow," she said. I realized for the first time that Mrs. Hudson's concern for Powder was not just on my account.

"Irresistible," I said.

"May I see the sign?"

I handed her one. She looked it over with a critical eye.

"Do you think the reward is enough?" She asked, handing me the sign back.

"Yeah, I think so. For most people, five hundred dollars is a whole lot of cash. You don't think it's enough?"

"I suppose it is," she said.

Then, as though she was thinking out loud, she added, "If

we don't get any results after a day or two, I will match it."

I set my coffee cup down.

"Mrs. Hudson, did you say we?"

She blushed slightly.

"I don't mean to be presumptuous," she said.

"You haven't been," I assured her. "I accept your gracious offer."

Now she fairly beamed.

I stood up.

"And now," I said. " I have some signs to put up. Thank you for the tea."

I finished tacking up my signs by two-thirty, and went back to the apartment. When I got there, I found Father Westcott sitting on the front porch, having lemonade with Mrs. Hudson. I walked up the steps.

"Father," I said.

He stood.

"Ah, Quinn. Mrs. Hudson said you would be back soon. I wanted to talk with you. Do you have a few minutes?"

I pocketed my keys.

"Certainly," I said.

Mrs. Hudson stood up and gathered the lemonade glasses onto a tray, which she carried to the door.

"I have some work to do inside, boys," she said.

"It was nice talking with you, Father, thank you very much," she said. She went inside.

I sat down, and gestured for Father Westcott to do the same.

He seemed slightly uncomfortable, but I didn't say anything. I was trying to figure out what he was doing here You usually find out more when you keep your mouth shut.

"I suppose you're wondering why I'm here," he said.

I nodded.

"Yes, well, it's about the other night."

"I thought it might be," I said.

He looked around to make sure Mrs. Hudson had gone inside and that the front door was closed.

"I think there's more going on than you told us," he said.

"Do you, now?"

"Yes, I do, and you know it already. So don't play dumb."

"Is that what I was doing? I thought I was just being careful about what I said, and waiting to see what you had to say."

He appeared agitated. I seemed to have that effect on people lately.

"There was a detective at the church this morning," he said finally.

I said nothing.

"His name was Ramsey," he said. He waited to see if this caused me to fall off my chair.

I didn't.

"Would you like to know what this Ramsey had to say?"

"I have a feeling you would like me to know what he said."

Westcott was gritting his teeth now. I could see his jaw muscles flexing.

"I can't figure you out, Black. I can't figure out if you're a good man, as Father O'Dell thinks you are, or if you're a vigilante, as Ramsey seems to think you are."

"He said that?" I asked.

"Not in so many words, but it wasn't difficult to figure out."

"Why don't you tell me what he did say, then," I suggested.

Westcott leaned in closer, putting his elbows on his knees. His breath smelled faintly of coffee.

"He said he noticed from a police report that you had been at the church when it was vandalized. He thought there might have been a connection between the vandalism and the man who killed your wife. He asked me if I knew anything about that."

Ramsey was smart, had to give him that.

I said, "So what did you tell him?"

Westcott looked annoyed.

"I told him nothing, because Father O'Dell wanted it that way. Father O'Dell did most of the talking."

"And what did Father O'Dell say?"

"He artfully danced around the truth. He didn't reveal anything that you told us that night."

I thought about this. It puzzled me that O'Dell would be so interested in protecting me. I didn't know what to make of it.

"And did Ramsey have anything else to say?"

"Yes, he did, and that's why I came to see you," Westcott said. "He said that you had been stalking this man. He said that you had been watching him. He said that he thought you might have been planning to do more than just watch."

He waited, obviously looking for a reaction, but I had none to offer him.

"He said he thought you might be planning to kill him."

"Do you think I'm planning to kill this man?"

Westcott looked me in the eye. I think he might have been trying to hypnotize me.

"Are you?" he asked.

I didn't answer him right away. This was getting slippery. If I didn't play this right, Ramsey might really keep us from doing the job. And I couldn't allow that to happen.

"Father," I said. "Look me in the eye."

I didn't really have to say that—he was already looking me in the eye. But it sounded good.

"I am not a murderer, nor do I plan to become one."

I said it with as much conviction as I could muster. I hoped it sounded sincere, because it was sincere. I didn't intend to become a murderer. I intended to dispense justice.

I was hoping that Father Westcott would hear what he wanted to hear in the words I said.

He leaned back in his chair and breathed a sigh of relief.

"I am so thankful to hear you say that," he said. "I have agonized about this."

I didn't respond.

"I talked to Father O'Dell about my fears that Ramsey was right. And that I was worried that he was trying to protect you. Which would be almost like helping you commit murder."

"Really?" I tried to sound nonchalant. "And what did he say?"

Father Westcott smiled sheepishly.

"He said I shouldn't be so quick to correct people for sins when I didn't even know if they had committed them."

"Father O'Dell is a wise man," I said.

"Yes. He is. He told me something that might be helpful to you," Westcott said. He sounded tentative, as if I might be offended.

"What was that?" I said.

"When I asked him whether he thought you might actually be considering murder, Father O'Dell said that God always exacts vengeance. But that He does it in His own way, and that we shouldn't interfere."

"I think I know just what he meant," I said quietly.

Father Westcott sat quietly for a while. Then he pointed to one of my reward signs hanging on a telephone pole across the street.

"Mrs. Hudson told me about your dog."

I shrugged.

"I hope you find him."

"Oh, don't worry," I said. "I'm persistent. I'll find him eventually."

Chapter 22

"Quinn, can you come over right away?" It was Robin Helton, and he sounded nervous.

"Did you find something on Angie's computer?"

"Just come over. You need to see this for yourself."

Robin ushered me into his house after doing a quick look up and down the block, and he locked the door behind us. Not his usual style.

"What is it, Rob?" I asked.

"Well," he said as he gestured to Angie's computer, which was open and turned on, sitting on Robin's dining room table. "There's a lot more than just a few encrypted emails on here. She was keeping a diary, but she had it hidden."

I sat down and looked at the screen, but couldn't bring myself to read anything on it just yet. I was still trying to process the idea that Angie had a secret diary. Secret from me.

"What's in it?" I asked.

Robin sat in a chair on the opposite side of the table, and lit a Chesterfield cigarette. He took a deep drag and expelled a cloud of blue smoke before answering me.

"Lot of stuff, bro. I stopped reading it once I realized it was, eh, very private. Stuff about some illegal real estate deals, and stuff about you, too."

I looked up from the laptop's screen and stared at Robin.

The skin across the back of my neck felt damp and cold.

"Stuff about me?"

He cleared his throat. "Yeah. Nothing bad, from what I saw. Mostly about her feeling guilty about not telling you about what she was messed up in."

He took another pull on his cigarette. I held out my hand, and he gave me the pack of smokes and his lighter. I lit a cigarette and started paging through the file on Angie's laptop.

She had been doing background work on some of Cerazini's real estate deals.

It had been part of her job. She had uncovered some very damning evidence of insurance fraud on Cerazini's part. She had decided not to tell anyone until she was certain—Angie hadn't wanted to ruin someone's life based on circumstantial evidence or assumptions she might have made.

I sighed, and closed the laptop. There was a lot more— she had been keeping this diary for months.

I decided I should read it later.

Robin was watching me without saying a word. I admired him for not speaking. Most people would have felt compelled to prattle on, to fill the awkward silence. Not Robin. He was unconventional in many ways. It's why I liked him.

I picked up the laptop and crushed out my cigarette.

"I only read enough to know I should stop reading," Robin said.

I nodded, and walked to the front door. He followed me, unlocked the door and held it open for me.

"Then I guess I forgot everything I had read," he said.

"That's best," I said.

I stepped outside.

"Call me sometime and let me know you're doing OK," Rob said.

"Deal."

I left with the laptop under my arm and a world of thoughts

flying through my head. Foremost among those thoughts: the idea that I was now certain of Cerazini's involvement in my wife's death.

Chapter 23

I drove to Dr. Bibb's office that afternoon and arrived early for my appointment. Dr. Bibbs was going over some notes with his receptionist and saw me come in the door. He smiled.

"Quinn, how are you?"

"Fine, I think," I said. "Why so cheerful?"

"I have some good news. Come on back. I had a no-show."

I followed him to his office. It was orderly as usual, though I noticed a file laying in the center of his desk. It was perfectly squared with the desktop. No papers poked from the edges of the file folder. Anyone who didn't believe in parallel worlds had never met Dr Bibbs, who lived in one; in his world, everything was parallel.

We sat, and he tapped on the folder with his index finger.

"I have some interesting reading for you, Quinn."

He smiled.

"And?"

"Well, you can read the details yourself, but the summary is that I have found at least three or four more case histories that are similar to yours. Each of theses cases," he slid the folder across the desk to me, "involves a patient who suffered a brain injury that deeply effected their ability to sleep. Two of them haven't slept for years."

I picked the file up, and flipped through it. It was thick. He was right; this was going to be interesting reading.

"Any other side effects?"

Bibbs nodded.

"Yes, but they vary from case to case, and only one is serious."

I looked up at him.

"Epilepsy. But so far you don't show any signs of that."

I scratched my head along the scar.

"What about these 'episodes' I keep having?"

Bibbs nodded again.

"It is possible that these are some kind of seizure, but we don't have any confirmation of that. The EEG shows nothing unusual. I suspect that maybe your 'episodes' are really panic attacks."

I thought about this. It didn't seem to ring true, but I didn't know how to argue the point, so I didn't.

"How is the meditation working for you?" he asked.

I shrugged.

"Can't tell, really. I'm working at it."

He tapped his fingers on the edge of the desk.

"Well, keep it up, Quinn. You might consider taking a class. Spokane Falls has one that starts this month."

I raised my eyebrows.

"How do you know this?"

He smiled.

"I checked. The information is in the back of that file. Meditation is very useful for patients with sleep disturbances, and I really want you to stick with it."

Perhaps I had been to hard on Dr. Bibbs in the past. Maybe he just wanted to keep the subject of his next journal article alive and kicking.

Whatever the case, he seemed to be doing his best to take good care of me.

"I will," I said. "And I'll read this tonight."

I stood, and shook his hand.

"Thanks, Doc."

I left his office thinking over the idea that I might live for a very long time without ever getting a good night's sleep.

Chapter 24

I met Ping at the gym, and we made the rounds: thirty minutes on the treadmill, a nice upper body workout in the free weight room, and then another thirty minutes on the treadmill. Nothing too rough—just maintenance, really.

After my shower, I looked myself over in the mirror, and was taken back by what I saw. It isn't that I was admiring my own form—far from it. I was surprised by the marks the last few months had left on me. The scars on my head were fading but still very visible under the fine stubble on my head. Since I had lost so much fat, my face looked gaunt and harsh as it never had before—my cheeks were starkly defined, and my eyes seemed a little sunken back into my head.

A scar was visible under my left nipple, a remnant of one of the procedures in the ER after I was shot. I turned slightly and could still see the faint bruise where one of Minor's boys had hit me across the back with a baseball bat.

I looked like a junk-yard dog. I got dressed and met Ping at the juice bar. We both ordered water.

"If we needed any more confirmation about Cerazini, we can both rest easy now," Ping said.

He reached into his gym bag on the floor next to his stool and pulled out a manila folder. He slid it along the counter without looking at me. His eyes were on a young blond woman working the treadmill directly across from us. She was tall, tan, and perfectly proportioned. I've never figured out whether coming to the gym makes them look this way, or whether it's only because they look this way that they're willing to come to the gym.

I tore my eyes away from Ms. Treadmill and opened the envelope. Inside were three sheets of paper, each showing a printout of an e-mail. The e-mails were about Angie—a discussion between Cerazini and someone whose name I didn't recognize.

The last email ended with this sentence: "The woman is going to blow the whole thing. I'm going to have her taken care of."

When I looked up at Ping, I know my eyes were filled with tears, but I managed to blink them back. Ping didn't say anything.

I told him about the laptop.

"Not much doubt about it now. Cerazini goes down too."

Ping nodded.

"Fine by me," he said. "Nobody will complain, I imagine."

He took a drink of water.

"It got pretty scary, didn't it?" he asked.

"Yeah, I guess," I said. "But my only real fear was failing."

"I know," he said.

I read the e-mails again, and then put them back in the folder.

"Can I keep these?"

"If you like," he said. "Can't see what I would use them for."

I nodded, and slipped the envelope into my own gym bag. The blond had stepped up the speed of the treadmill, with delightful results. I felt a small pang of guilt for looking. But the truth is, it was only a small one. Some things don't change, I guess.

Eddy Solomon, the guy who handles the physical therapy cases for the gym, came shuffling over and sat down beside Ping.

"Hey, Quinn, how's it doing?" he said.

"It's been worse," I answered. Eddy was probably a little insulted that I had never come to him for therapy, despite the severity of my injuries.

I'd like to say I felt guilty about that, but the truth is Eddy gave me the creeps. He was a stocky little guy, very hairy, with dark brown kinky hair. He had more hair on the back of his knuckles than most men had on their heads. He had a habit of breathing with his mouth open, which only added to the illusion that he was in fact a well-trained ape.

"Getting back to normal, dude?" he asked. He nodded his head, as if answering his own question.

"Yeah, Eddy," I said, nodding my head in unison with his, "I sure am."

He chewed on his bottom lip for a moment, and then said, "Did that guy ever find you?"

Ping's eyebrows went up, but he still didn't look up at Eddy. Eddy creeped Ping out even more than he did me.

"What guy would that be?" I said.

"Guy was in here looking for you the other day, dude. Wouldn't give his name. About as tall as you, light-colored hair. Blue suit."

Ah. Ramsey.

Ping looked at me.

I shrugged, and said, "Probably my insurance agent."

"Oh," Eddy said, as if it might have been any of his business.

"Tell you what Eddy," I said. "If he comes back, tell him that I went to Hawaii for a vacation. And give him a massage, will you? Tell him he looks tense. I'll pay for it."

Eddy smiled—always glad to earn a dollar. And to feel up

some strange guy, unless I missed my guess.

"No problem, Quinn. You don't want him to find you, huh?"

Eddy's lack of a clue never ceased to amaze me. He just didn't get the fact that this was none of his business.

Ping said, "Honorable Quinn owe him money."

I hated it when Ping did his cheesy Chinese Accent. I might have found it less offensive if he had ever really had a Chinese accent to begin with.

Eddy grinned. It was a mischievous, we're-in-it-together kind of grin. It made me want to punch him in the mouth.

"Gotcha," he said. "I'll do just like you said."

He got up and wandered off, scanning the gym for other victims, no doubt. I looked at Ping and tried my best to show my disgust on my face.

"Honorable Quinn?" I said. "Don't you ever get tired of that?"

He put his hands together and bowed slightly.

"No," he said.

Some people are beyond hope.

We sat there for a while longer, and finally Ping crumpled up his paper water cup and stood.

"Let's take a walk," he said.

The night air was cool, especially after the workout and shower. We threw our stuff in the car, and began to stroll along the sidewalk down Regal Street, which runs north-south down the South Hill. Despite the cool air, quite a few people were out that night, walking their dogs and their sweethearts—in some cases, I suspected they were one and the same.

"OK," I said. "Here's the way I see it. We need to wait, but not too long."

"Right," Ping said. He sounded as if he might be grading my plan for me.

"After things cool down a bit, we just watch until we can catch them together."

"Right."

I shrugged, and said, "And then we pop them."

Ping stopped walking, and looked at me.

"Did you say 'pop them'?" he asked.

I stopped too, and stared right back at him.

"Yeah, I did."

"OK, G-Man, just checking," he said, and resumed walking.

I was slightly ruffled at the not-so-subtle mockery, but I let it slide. He was, after all, assisting me in my revenge plan.

"Think we can do it without getting caught?" I asked.

"I'd give us fifty-fifty odds," he answered.

That seemed good enough for me. We turned around and headed back to the car.

Chapter 25

I went home and sat on the couch. My head was pounding a little, so I got up and swallowed four aspirin. I chewed them, but the bitter taste was more than I could stand, so I drank a bottle of Amber Ale to wash the taste out of my mouth.

I turned on the TV, but after making the round of channels twice, I gave up and turned it off. How could there be a hundred and thirty-seven channels and still nothing worth watching? I decided that I would have the cable disconnected tomorrow. Why pay for something I not only didn't use, but actually found annoying?

I sat in the dark looking at the faint afterglow on the TV screen.

I sank back into the couch and did the counting routine Dr. Bibbs had taught me—from a hundred down to zero, visualizing a staircase in my mind. With each number, I pictured myself taking another step downward, until I reached the bottom.

My thoughts smoothed out into what I had come to recognize as alpha state. I felt completely relaxed, but I could still hear the ticking of the alarm clock in the next room, the buzz of the refrigerator, and the occasional barking of a dog down the street.

It wasn't sleep, but it was as close to rest as I could get. I drank it in.

I'm not sure exactly how long I sat there like that, but it must have been several hours. I was conscious of more light in the room—meaning the sun was rising—and then I heard a soft knock at the door.

I opened my eyes, wide awake as ever.

"Quinn?" Mrs. Hudson's voice came through the door. "Quinn, are you awake?"

I laughed and got up, went over and opened the door.

"Yes, Mrs. Hudson, I am."

I looked at my watch. Eight a.m.

She was wearing her usual semi-dressy outfit, complete with jewelry and low-heeled shoes, even though I was pretty sure she had no plan to go anywhere today.

"Would you like to come in?" I asked.

She was smiling.

"No, but perhaps you could come down stairs. We may have some information on Powder."

I grabbed my keys and wallet from the tray by the door and followed her downstairs, locking the apartment behind me.

A tall, skinny boy with acne across his forehead and cheeks stood in the parlor. He was wearing a long green tee-shirt that said "Go Army" across the front, faded baggy jeans, and clunky work boots.

He had one of my signs in his hand, and held it up when I entered the room.

"This your dog?" he said.

I nodded.

"Yeah, he's mine. Do you have him?"

The kid shook his head.

"Nope, but I think I may have seen him down behind Rosaeur's."

I thought for a moment. Rosaeur's grocery was a couple of streets down and over from us—it was very conceivable that Powder might have been there looking for food.

"When?" I asked, moving toward the door.

The kid shrugged.

"Couple days ago, I guess," he said.

I grabbed him by the arm and said, "Come on, you can show me."

We stepped out the front door when the kid stopped and said, "You ain't a weirdo, are you?"

Some questions never lose their charm.

"Not the last time I checked," I said.

The kid appeared to be thinking. It seemed to be a process he was unaccustomed to.

"I want my reward money," he said.

I shook my head.

"No reward until I find the dog."

He stared at me defiantly.

"Well?" I said. "Do you want the money or not?"

He shrugged again—he seemed more comfortable with the shrugging than with the thinking—and followed me down the steps to the car.

As I got in, I turned to Mrs. Hudson, who was still standing on the steps.

"I'll be back as soon as I can," I said. "Maybe I'll bring him with me!"

She smiled and waved as we drove away.

The trip proved to be a bust.

I drove around with the kid—a high school freshman named Nate VanAndel—for about 45 minutes, but we didn't turn up any sign of Powder.

I told Nate that if I found Powder and it seemed likely at all that his information had been accurate, I would pay him his reward.

Hell, I had a million-dollar check on the way, didn't I?

I drove slowly back to Mrs. Hudson's place, looking back and forth for any sign of my dog, but no luck.

I parked the car and went inside, and found Mrs. Hudson in the kitchen, drying some dishes.

She set down the glass and her dishtowel, and rushed over to the kitchen doorway, looking past me into the dining room.

"Did you find him?" she asked.

I sat at the dining room table and sighed.

"No, it was a wild geese chase," I said.

She made a pouting face. When she was younger, Mrs. Hudson had probably been one heck of a heartbreaker.

"Goose," she said.

"What?"

"You mean a wild goose chase," she said. She sat down across from me. "I am very disappointed."

"Me too," I said.

"Oh, dear, I almost forgot," she said and began checking the pockets of her apron for something.

"Forgot what?" I asked.

"Father Westcott came by earlier," she said. "He came to see you, and I told him he should wait and that you would be back soon. So we talked on the porch for a few minutes. And then the other man."

She found what she was looking for, a small folded slip of paper, and waved it in front of me victoriously.

"The other man came, and they left together."

"Other man?" She had my full attention now.

"Yes, such a nice young man, he said that he knew you and he was going to take Father Westcott and they would try to find you."

"What was this man's name?" I asked. "Was it O'Dell?"

"No," she said. "Here."

My heart was racing now. If not O'Dell, then who? I swallowed and tried to appear calm.

She handed me the slip of paper.

"I wrote it down, along with his phone number. He said if

he didn't find you, you should call him tonight," she said.

I held the paper for a moment, not wanting to look at it. I already knew what I would find.

I looked down.

Written on the paper, in Mrs. Hudson's spidery script, was the name I had expected: Danny Minor.

Chapter 26

I excused myself from Mrs. Hudson and went upstairs and called Ping's number. No answer. He didn't use an answering machine, so I couldn't leave a message. I was going to have to go over, and there was no guarantee he would be there when I arrived.

I looked at the note Minor had left, and realized I was going to have to call him. I swallowed and picked up the phone.

"Yeah," he answered.

"It's Quinn Black," I said.

"Black. Good. I have your friend here. He really wants to see you."

I didn't say anything.

"Cat got your tongue, Black?"

"What do you want?" I said.

"I think you know what I want, pal."

"You want me dead."

"Bingo. I figure you don't want to cooperate with that idea, but I have your priest friend here. If you don't give yourself up to me, I'm going to kill him."

"What makes you think I'm willing to die for him?"

"Well, I thought of that," he said. "I figure if you want to play it like that, I'll kill him anyway and we'll see if that changes your mind. Because if it don't, I'm coming for the old lady next."

"What's to stop me from bringing in the cops?" I asked. I was stalling for time, trying to think of the right things to say. What the hell were the right things to say? I had no idea what Minor might really want or what he might really do.

"Because you don't want me arrested, Black. You want me dead, and you want to do it yourself. So you'll play along."

He took a deep breath.

"And pal, let me tell you—I want you dead, too. The truth is I'm just trying to make it easy on myself. But you are going to die, one way or the other. Or maybe you'll kill me. Either way, you'll have to come meet me on my terms. I'll be calling you later to set something up."

"And you're sure I'll be there?"

"Yeah, because you're stupid enough to believe you might still find a way out of this," he said, and then he hung up.

The thing that frustrated me was he was right.

I called Ping again, and this time he answered on the third ring.

"I just got off the phone with Danny Minor," I said.

"You guys phone buddies now?"

"He's kidnapped Father Westcott," I said. "He says he's going to call back and set up some kind of exchange—me for Westcott."

"You realize the idea is to kill you, right?"

"Yeah," I said. "I figured that part out. What Minor doesn't know is that I have a different plan in mind."

"Oh, I think he does know that," Ping said, "Which is why we need to be very careful right now. I'm coming over. And I'm bringing some backup."

"Backup?" I said.

"Friend of mine. He was in the Gulf."

"Can we trust this guy?"

"I think so." He hung up.

I waited.

I was on the front porch smoking a cigarette when Ping's car pulled up on the street. I had the cordless phone stuck in my shirt pocket, so I wouldn't miss Minor's call.

Ping got out of the car, and Father O'Dell got out of the passenger side.

I said, "This is your backup?"

O'Dell nodded. He was wearing jeans and sneakers, and a short-sleeved back shirt with a priest's collar.

I shook my head as they came up the steps.

"No way," I said.

O'Dell grabbed my arm by the bicep. His grip was not weak.

"Listen to me," he said. "I am responsible for that man being in this situation. I put him at risk. I will not abandon him now."

"No, you'll get us all killed," I said. I looked at Ping. "I can't believe you think this is a good idea. This is going to screw up the whole operation."

"I don't think so," O'Dell said. He backed away from me, turned his back to me for a moment, and then turned to face me again.

He handed me the pieces of my Glock, which he had apparently taken from my belt and field-stripped in a matter of a few seconds.

"OK, your sleight-of-hand is good," I said. "But are you prepared to shoot someone today if the need arises?"

"No. I am not prepared to do violence on any of the Lord's children. But my guess is that there will be more things to do on this little venture than shooting or hitting people. I can serve as a distraction. I can be a peacemaker. I can do surveillance. I am prepared to do what it takes—short of taking a life—to rescue

Father Westcott," he said. "That should be enough."

I looked at Ping, who shrugged.

"I wouldn't have brought him if I didn't think he could handle it," Ping said.

"How do you know he can?"

"Gut feeling."

I looked from Ping to Father O'Dell and back again.

"And you didn't think that was worth mentioning to me, or discussing with me?" I asked.

Ping shrugged again.

"It never came up," he said.

"Now, what's the plan?" O'Dell said.

I finished re-assembling my weapon.

"Why don't we get off this porch?" Ping said.

We went back upstairs to my apartment. Ping came in the door last, but left it open and stood just inside the frame, so he could watch the stairs.

"Here's what I think we should do," he said. While he was talking, he took his own gun from under his jacket, ejected the clip, reinserted it, disengaged the safety, and re-holstered it. Ready-check, he called it.

"Ready-check saves lives," I said with a smile.

Ping smiled back, and said, "We wait for Minor to call. Get the details of the setup, and then we go to the meeting, We'll all ride in Quinn's car. I'll ride in the passenger seat, so I'm visible."

O'Dell raised a finger.

"Why give away your presence?" he said.

"Because Minor will be expecting Ping to be around," I said. "If he's not visible, they'll be more inclined to look the vehicle over. And since you'll be hiding in the back, we don't want them looking too closely."

Ping gestured toward me with a "there you have your answer" motion.

O'Dell grunted.

"And what if they just fill the car full of bullet holes without bothering to check?" he asked. I thought it was a fair question.

"Then I'm glad we'll have our priest along," Ping said. "Because we will most certainly be dead."

"I don't think they'll try that, though," I said.

"Why not?" O'Dell raised an eyebrow.

"Because once they kill us—and they are planning to kill us, by their own admission—they will need to dispose of the bodies. A car full of blood and bullet holes is too much trouble to dump. Better for them if they can get us to come with them. Then they can shoot us somewhere convenient."

"You seem to know a lot about these things," Father O'Dell said.

Ping said nothing, and O'Dell looked at me.

"I don't ask," I said.

The phone rang, and we all looked at one another. It rang a second time, and I answered.

"Black," I said.

"Quinn, this is Stan Ramsey."

I pressed the mute button on the phone and said, "It's Ramsey, don't say anything," and then pressed the mute button again.

"Yeah, what's up, Ramsey?"

"I was wondering if I could stop by and talk for a few minutes?"

"Why would you want to come by here? What's on your mind?"

O'Dell was shaking his head, and Ping's eyebrows went up. I figured that made it unanimous—none of us wanted Ramsey dropping in right now.

"I've got some interesting news," Ramsey said. "Thought you might like to know about it."

There was something odd about the way Ramsey was talking to me,

"Really?" I said. "Can't you tell me over the phone? I was just getting ready to leave. I have an appointment."

I went over to the window and twisted the handle to open the blinds slightly. I looked down the street and saw a plain white Chevy Caprice turning the corner.

"I'd really rather tell you in person, Quinn," Ramsey said.

I hung up the phone and tossed it onto the sofa.

"What is it?" Ping asked.

"Ramsey was stalling," I said. "He's going to pull up in front of the house in about thirty seconds."

"We can't leave here until we get the call from Minor," Ping said.

"I can forward the calls to my cell-phone," I said. I snatched up the phone and started dialing, setting up the forwarding as we all clamored down the steps. We went through the kitchen and out the back door. I was parked behind the house.

We piled into the car, and I tossed the cordless phone into the back seat. My cell phone was on my belt. I glanced down to make sure the cell phone's power was on, saw the little green LED flash on and off, then I started the car and drove straight across Mrs. Hudson's purple mums, through the neighbors' back yard, and out the other side onto 32nd Avenue.

"With any luck," Ping said, "He didn't see us pull out."

"I don't think we can count on that," O'Dell said. "Can't this car go any faster?"

I circled around and drove onto High Drive, which took us right past the corner where we could see Mrs. Hudson's place. I caught a glimpse of Ramsey getting out of his car and walking toward the porch, where Mrs. Hudson was standing with a tray of ice tea and smiling.

I found myself smiling as I turned my attention back to the

road.

"What are you grinning about?" O'Dell asked.

"My accomplice—Mrs. Hudson—will keep Ramsey busy for a while," I said.

O'Dell looked puzzled, but Ping laughed.

Chapter 27

My cell phone rang after we had been driving for about twenty minutes. We were cruising down Sprague Avenue, past a few pawn shops, one tattoo parlor, and a used CD store. My phone rang again.

I answered it.

"This is Black," I said.

"Have you had time to call your Jap buddy yet?" Minor's voice, and his impeccable manners, were unmistakable.

"Yes," I said. Why lie?

"I figured you would want to bring him in on this," Minor said. "Just know this: if you bring in the cops, I'm going to pop a cap into the choirboy, here."

"No police," I said.

"All right," Minor said. "Listen up. I'm only saying this one time."

"I'm listening," I said.

"We'll meet tonight at midnight in State Line."

State Line was a scruffy little town just across the Washington-Idaho border, about a half-hour drive from downtown Spokane.

"Where in State Line?" I said.

"I'll tell you that tonight. There's a phone booth right next to the strip bar there," he said. "Do you know where that is?"

"Yes."

"Yeah, I figured you would. You rich boys are never as clean as you like to pretend you are."

I literally bit my tongue and said nothing.

"I'll be calling that pay phone tonight at about midnight," Minor said. "Make sure you're there to answer it."

He hung up.

I kept driving, traveling east on Sprague Avenue, and eventually pulled into the parking lot of the Thunderbird Inn.

On the way, I recounted my conversation with Minor.

"Why all the cloak and dagger?" O'Dell said.

Ping slapped the dash. He was shaking his head.

"He's got Cerazini with him," he said.

"Why do you say that?" I said.

"Who is Cerazini?" O'Dell asked.

Ping said, "He's Minor's boss. Cerazini ordered Minor to kill Angie."

"So why do you think Cerazini is there?" I asked.

"Is Minor smart enough to come up with this routine?" Ping asked.

I shook my head.

"No, probably not." I said.

"Right. Cerazini is smart enough. And he's also smart enough to know that the odds are probably even on how we'll handle this. He has no way of knowing you won't call the police in, even though he told you not to."

"So he's being careful just to avoid being arrested," O'Dell said.

Ping nodded.

"Which means they'll both be there tonight," I said.

Ping nodded again.

"Outstanding," I said.

O'Dell leaned over the back seat.

"Are we planning to rescue Father Westcott, or is there some other thing you have in mind?"

I looked at O'Dell.

"We'll get Father Westcott," I said. "Anything else that goes down, you don't have to worry about."

"I don't like the sound of that, Quinn," he said.

"Then do your best not to listen, Father."

I got out and went into the Thunderbird office to get us a room.

We needed a place to hide out for the next ten hours. It wouldn't do to get picked up by Ramsey before we could finish our business.

The teenager behind the front desk no doubt was having all sorts of lurid ideas about three men checking into a hotel room together at this time of day—but I didn't bother to try and explain anything to him.

I paid cash for the room, took the key, and decided to go to the men's room in the lobby before I went back out to the car.

I walked into the men's room, and as I opened the door I felt as if I were falling through a tunnel into a large black space. I tried to scream, but no sound came out. I heard a loud noise. Then all was dark and quiet, and I was floating in the void.

I opened my eyes and saw a lumpy white surface.

At first I thought it might be the surface of the moon, but then I saw the cheap light fixture to the left and realized it was a ceiling.

I rolled my head to the left, and saw Father O'Dell reading a Gideon's Bible. I raised myself up on my elbows.

Ping was seated on the bed next to me, watching CNN.

"Ah," said O'Dell, "You have returned."

"Yeah," I said. "What happened?"

Ping shut off the TV and turned around to face me.

"You tell us. All we know is the kid in the lobby came running out to the car saying you had passed out in the john."

I got to my feet. I didn't feel dizzy. My left arm hurt a

little. I must have smacked it when I went down.

"I don't really know what happened," I said.

"Something to do with your injury?" Ping pointed to his head, as if I might have needed help figuring out what he meant.

"Yeah," I said. I shook my head and took a deep breath. "But I'm fine now. How long was I out?"

Ping looked at his watch.

"Less than fifteen minutes."

He squinted at me and pursed his lips.

"What?" I said. It wasn't hard to see that he was thinking hard about something, and I knew that something was me.

"Well, what if you have one of your fainting spells tonight?" Ping asked.

"I won't."

O'Dell said, "How do you know?"

"Because I can't afford to, that's how."

Ping made a smacking sound with his lips.

"Good," he said. "I'm glad that's cleared up."

Ping, the master of subtle sarcasm.

Chapter 28

We spent the rest of the day watching CNN and taking turns at the window looking for signs that anyone had followed us to the hotel. There was also the chance that the kid at the desk had called us in as suspicious characters, but I was guessing the Thunderbird catered mostly to suspicious characters. Chances are we were just about normal as far as Thunderbird clientele goes.

Ping produced a pack of playing cards—I have no idea where he got them—and we played poker for a couple of hours.

At about eight, after the sun had set, I suggested maybe we should get something to eat.

"Right," Ping said. "We don't want you passing out from hunger."

I did my best to look angry with him, but I knew he was really asking me how I felt.

"That's not going to happen," I said.

I wish I could have been as nonchalant as I sounded. I didn't know why I had passed out earlier, and there had been no warning.

I assumed it was somehow related to my sleep disorder—but it had been so long since I'd had any problems in that regard that I wasn't completely sure.

"I'll go for food," O'Dell said.

I pulled a fifty from my pocket and handed it to him.

"There's a burger place down the street a couple of blocks," I said. "Ronn's, or something like that."

O'Dell stood up and stuffed the money in his pocket. I liked the fact that he didn't make a big deal out of who would pay for the food. Most men would.

"Burgers, fries and Cokes?" he asked.

I nodded, and Ping stood up.

"I think I'd better go with you," Ping said.

O'Dell looked surprised.

"Rough neighborhood for a priest," Ping said.

They stood looking at one another for a moment.

"Joke," I said to O'Dell. "You haven't known him long enough to realize it yet, but that was a joke."

"Ah," O'Dell said.

Ping opened the door, and O'Dell glanced at me.

"I'm fine," I said.

They left, and I sat on the bed. What are we doing? I wondered. What was wrong with me—would I space out at some critical moment and get us all killed?

I realized I was willing to take the risk—any risk, to anyone—if it would bring me justice for Angie. If it would mean the death of Danny Minor and Cerazini.

When Ping and O'Dell returned, we ate in silence. It's an odd thing, but it was some of the best food I ever ate—the burgers were greasy, and the flavor of the grill blended seamlessly with the fresh onion and tomato. The fries were crisp and still steamy hot, glistening with salt.

We finished eating, gathered up our belongings, and checked our weapons. Father O'Dell was absently fingering his rosary beads.

I checked my watch. It was 11:05 p.m.

We left the hotel and went around back to the car. I never

even saw the white Chevy, which must have been just across the street—at least until later.

Chapter 29

We drove to State Line; it took about thirty minutes. As we exited from the interstate to the off-ramp, I said, "Better lie down, Father. They're probably watching for us."

O'Dell sunk down onto the back seat, and I pulled up in front of the phone booth at around 11:40. I parked right next to it and cracked the window a smidgen, so we could hear the phone if it rang. Then I switched off the car and we sat in the dark, listening to the ticking of the engine.

Just down the street, the parking lot of State Line Showgirls was almost full. One lone street light illumined the lot. It wasn't enough, and most of the lot was lost in the gray shadows. It occurred to me that most of the guys inside probably didn't want the parking lot well lit.

I lit a cigarette. Ping grimaced. I offered the pack to O'Dell but he refused. We sat there for another fifteen minutes, and the phone rang.

I got out of the car and answered it.

"You're early. That's good," Minor said.

"What now?"

"Look down the road, to the east," he said. "Do you see the stop sign?"

It was about a half-mile from us, barely visible.

"Yeah."

"Turn left at the sign, go about two miles. You'll see a driveway with a mailbox at the end."

"OK," I said.

"Name on the box is Mullins. Drive up to the house. Get out of the car. If you wait too long, we'll shoot this faggot and then we'll shoot you and your Jap friend. Got it?"

"How do I know you didn't already shoot Father Westcott?"

"You don't," he said. I heard the click as he hung up.

I got in the car and relayed the conversation to Ping and O'Dell.

"Let me out," O'Dell said. I looked at him.

"What?"

"Let me out at the end of the driveway. I have a feeling they're going to check the car, or shoot it full of holes anyway. I don't want to be inside. Plus, if I can approach the house from the driveway, maybe I can surprise them."

"Maybe," I said. "There's a lot we don't know. If there's no cover around the driveway, we can't let you out. They may have someone watching, either way. We don't know if they plan to shoot us the instant we step out of the car. Or while we're driving up to the house."

"I thought you said it would be too messy to dispose of a car full of blood and bullet holes," Father O'Dell said.

"Yeah, but he could be wrong," Ping said.

"And don't forget this is Idaho," I said. "There's a lot of places to hide a car in this state. It might not be as tough as we thought."

I started the car and pulled onto the road, and as I did an idea occurred to me.

"Father, could you tell me if there's a baseball bat back there in the floor?"

"Yes, there is," he said.

I smiled.

Outstanding.

We turned onto the small two-lane road at the stop sign, and I reset the trip meter on the dash to zero.

The road was unlit, with woods on both sides. Perfect. The trees would offer plenty of cover.

I slowed down a bit.

"All right," I said. "I have a slight change of plans. Here's what we're going to do."

I explained it all to them, and nobody argued with me.

As we made the turn at the mailbox, I had the headlights set on bright beam.

"Are you sure you want to do it this way?" Ping said.

"I think it's our best chance."

Father O'Dell leaned over the back seat. There was no reason for him to hide now.

"Let's just do it," he said. He handed me the baseball bat, and I laid it along side my leg, right next to the gas pedal.

We crept up the driveway. Lucky for us it was long one—about a quarter mile, with a little farmhouse at the end of the driveway. A yellow bug-light glowed by the front door.

We moved at about three miles per hour. I wedged the bat onto the accelerator pedal gently, keeping the speed of the car constant. I looked up—nobody was on the porch, but there was a car parked beside the house.

I couldn't tell if anyone was in the car, but if so, I would just have to hope that the high beams from my car would prevent them from seeing what came next.

"Let's go," I said, and we all three opened our doors, hopped out, and shut the doors as we ran alongside in a crouch.

The car rolled on. We stayed low and ran just behind it.

The front door of the house opened, and three men stepped out.

I hoped the car would continue moving in a straight line. The devil is in the details.

Chapter 30

Our guns were drawn, and as we ran behind the car we kept low. The three men on the porch raised their weapons, aiming at the car, which was still creeping steadily toward the house straight ahead.

One of the men pointed his gun right at me. They had seen us.

None of the men on the porch looked familiar. Where was Minor?

The biggest of the three, the one who saw me first, stepped forward and started shooting. The other two joined suit.

Ping's weapon thundered beside me, and one of the three went down.

Ping was shouting something at me, but I couldn't hear what he was saying. I aimed at one of the two men remaining on the porch and fired, and his chest erupted in blood as he fell backwards and slumped against the front wall of the house.

I had been thinking over the last weeks about whether I had what it took to really shoot someone—and I found that in the moment it was easy. It was instinct. Survival.

My car bumped against the one parked in the driveway just as the doors of that car opened. Minor and a well-dressed man—I assumed Cerazini— stepped out, both of them just now realizing what was happening.

Minor pointed his pistol and shot, but I couldn't see who he was shooting at.

There was a flash of light and I looked over my shoulder. Another car was coming up the drive.

A round of shots banged out over our heads, and I dove into the weeds by the side of the driveway. I looked around.

Two of Minor's men were down, probably for good, but the third was nowhere to be seen. That had me worried.

My car butted nose first against Minor's car, the engine still groaning. The bat must still be wedged against the accelerator, I thought.

Minor and Cerazini had vanished around the corner of the house. The front door of the house was standing open, but it was dark inside.

I looked across the driveway and saw O'Dell crouched in the grass. He was motioning toward the driveway closer to the house.

I squinted into the gloom but could see nothing. The headlights from the car coming up the drive shined onto the form of a body lying in the driveway.

It was Ping.

The approaching car swerved around Ping and stopped in front of him, between the house and Ping. It was a white Chevy. The driver's door opened, and as the driver got out I pointed my gun at him.

He looked right at me and said, "Don't shoot me, you idiot! Help me!"

It was Ramsey.

He was rushing over to Ping. I followed quickly. O'Dell came across from the other side of the driveway. Ping wasn't conscious, but he was still alive. He'd been hit in the gut. No way to tell how bad it was. Gut shot's are no good, I knew that.

"Get him in the car," Ramsey said.

We lifted him up, and there was a fountain of blood from his mid-section.

"Good Lord," O'Dell said. We put Ping into the back seat. Ramsey looked at me.

"Your friend here is dying, if he isn't dead already. We need to get him to the hospital."

Father O'Dell said, "We're not leaving without Father Westcott."

"Do they have him?" Ramsey asked.

I nodded.

"Jesus Christ," Ramsey said. He checked his clip. "Let's go," he said. He looked at me and his anger was easy to read. "As soon as we're done, you're under arrest."

Chapter 31

O'Dell ran to the left side of the house, Ramsey crept in through the front door, and I ran around to the right.

As I rounded the corner at the back of the house, I almost smacked into a tall thin man with slicked back hair. He turned around to look at me, and I put the muzzle of my gun under his nose.

"Michael Cerazini?" I said.

He didn't speak, so I nudged him with the gun. This is a very persuasive technique.

"Yes," he said.

I looked into his eyes. He was afraid—I could see tears forming. Was I really going to do this? This wasn't like what had happened out front. I wasn't defending myself now. I had him at my mercy. Ramsey wasn't here to stop me.

I watched a tear roll down his pale cheek. I thought about Angie.

"My wife's name," I said.

"What?" His voice came out as a whisper.

"Tell me my wife's name."

He sobbed, and I pressed the gun hard into his lip, pushing his head against the wall.

"Angela Black," he whispered.

I shot him.

Chapter 32

O'Dell rounded the corner.

He looked at the body on the ground at my feet.

"Did you see the other one?" I said.

"No," he said. He bent down next to Cerazini, making the sign of the cross.

"Father," I said.

He looked up.

"We don't have time, and he doesn't deserve it," I said.

He didn't hesitate, but he finished quickly, and then nodded his head and stood up. What was I going to do, shoot him?

He looked very pale. "Quinn, please. No more killing."

"Let's go in," I said.

We ran around to the front of the house and stepped in the front door.

There was no light in the living room, but the glow of the bug-light on the front porch illuminated the room enough for us to see.

The living room was empty except for a shabby couch, an end table with a lamp, and a straight-backed chair.

Tied to the chair, with a gag in his mouth, was Father Westcott. He stared at us with wide eyes, shaking his head back and forth. I had seen enough bad television to know that this meant Danny Minor was in the room.

I looked around, and saw two men outlined in the shadowy doorway leading to the next room. One was Ramsey. He was behind Danny Minor. They stepped forward into the living room, and I could see the relief on Westcott's face, though it took me a moment to figure out why.

Minor was wearing handcuffs.

Ramsey shoved him into the room. Minor stumbled and then regained his footing. He stood staring at me.

Once O'Dell realized that Minor was in custody and no longer a threat, he removed Westcott's gag.

"Father Westcott, are you OK?" O'Dell asked.

"Yes," Westcott said. He looked at Minor.

"There are five of them. Did you get them all?"

Ramsey looked at me, and I looked at O'Dell.

"Two men were shot as we drove up." He drew a breath. "They're dead, I think." O'Dell said.

"Cerazini is dead too," I said. I said it to Minor, who was watching me carefully. I became aware that I was walking toward him, my gun raised.

There was a gunshot, and Ramsey's head whipped around. He fell to the floor, but as he fell, he managed to squeeze off a round into the large man standing just outside the front door—the man who had just shot Ramsey from behind.

The big man in the doorway fell backward. He wouldn't be getting back up. Ever.

I looked toward Ramsey, but as I did Westcott screamed, "Look out!"

I ducked as Minor swung at me with both his fists together, trying to strike me with the edges of the handcuffs. I swept my leg under his, and he landed on his back on the floor. I stepped back and pointed my gun at him.

"Go ahead!" he screamed. "Go ahead, you chicken-shit! Do it!"

I squatted beside him and placed the gun at his temple.

He glared at me. It was the second time in my life I had seen pure, raw, hatred and evil in a human face. Ironically, the first time it had been on the same man's face.

I could smell his rotten breath as he smiled and said, "You don't have the balls."

"That," I said, "is where you're wrong."

I squeezed the trigger, and watched his brains spray across the wall.

I wish I could say I found the sight disturbing.

Chapter 33

Blue lights and sirens flooded the driveway outside. Ramsey must have radioed for backup before he came in, I thought.

I went over to check him. He was breathing normally. I looked at his head, and saw there was a long gash across his forehead, just above the eyebrows. The bullet had grazed his forehead and glanced off his skull. He was probably going to be just fine.

Outside, I heard several cars come to a halt on the gravel.

A voice from a loudspeaker said, "This is the police. Throw out your weapons and come out with your hands above your head."

O'Dell finished untying Father Westcott and helped him to his feet.

"Okay boys, let's do as the man says."

I tossed my weapon out the door.

We put up our hands and went out.

Slowly.

The ambulances arrived a few minutes later. Ramsey was wheeled out on a gurney, and the ambulance driver turned on the siren as they tore out.

I was sitting in the back of a police cruiser when the

helicopter arrived for Ping. He had nearly bled to death in the back of Ramsey's car.

The door of the cruiser opened and two officers pulled me out of the car. One of them I knew—Sheriff Jamie Mills. I had spent the last hour with him, answering his questions about how we had come here to rescue Father Westcott and how Ramsey had followed us.

"The priest verifies your story. Said it was self-defense."

I didn't say anything. I really hadn't known how O'Dell would tell the story.

Sheriff Mills spat on the ground.

"I still think there's something missing, but so far I haven't figured it out," he said.

"Is my friend going to be all right?" I asked.

"If you were so worried about your friend, you shouldn't have drug him out here," Mills said. "But to answer your question, I don't know. They're taking him to Sacred Heart."

He turned and left, talking to someone on his radio as he walked.

About a dozen police cars lined the driveway. Floodlights had been set up. A generator was buzzing. A photographer was flashing pictures of the bodies on the front porch.

I could hear about a half-dozen different radios chattering.

I saw O'Dell and Westcott approaching. Westcott was drinking coffee. He had a blanket around his shoulders.

"Hello, Father," I said.

Westcott said nothing.

"They say we have to go in to the station to fill out a complete statement," O'Dell said.

"Yeah, me too," I answered.

"After that, I guess we all get to go home," said Westcott. There was a hint of accusation in his tone, but I chose to ignore it.

"I wish that were true," I said.

Chapter 34

Ping sat looking out the hospital window at the air conditioning unit on the roof across the way.

"You'd think they could have given me a room with a better view," he said.

"You ungrateful bastard," I said.

"I suppose that's true."

He reached up and checked the level of fluid in his IV.

"About an hour till my next refill," he said.

We sat quietly for a moment.

"So how come you're not in jail?" he asked.

Ping, master of tact.

I looked out the window now. Another gray day, but I really didn't care. I was just glad to be here, talking to my friend.

"I'm sorry I got you mixed up in this," I said.

"My decision," he said.

"I guess."

I sighed.

"O'Dell and Westcott backed my story," I said.

"Self defense?"

"Yeah," I answered.

"And that's going to fly?"

"Looks that way," I said.

"How's Ramsey?" he asked.

"Oh, he's fine. They stitched him up and he was home in three days. He'll probably get a medal."

The nurse came in, checked Ping's pulse and his I.V., and left. She never spoke.

"You really bring out the best in people, don't you?" I said.

"It's a gift," he said. "How did Ramsey find us, anyway?"

"He says he saw us leaving Mrs. Hudson's, and radioed ahead. One of the city units saw us going into the Thunderbird. He staked us out and followed us—he wasn't really sure what we were up to."

"That'll teach him," Ping said.

I sat there until he had fallen asleep, and then I left.

Chapter 35

I drove to the cemetery with the window rolled down, even though it was about thirty degrees outside. I needed something to keep me focused, so I wouldn't collapse under the weight of my grief. I missed Angie as much right now as I ever had. I was teetering on the edge of the wound that had opened when Angie died. I suspected it would never heal.

The gates were open. There didn't seem to be many people at the cemetery today. I drove to the back and up the small hill, and parked near Angie's grave.

I got out of the car, walked across the narrow blacktop, and as I came around the tree I stopped dead in my tracks.

There, lying curled up in a little shivering ball, was Powder.

I fell to my knees and wept. I cried out without any thought of what I must have sounded like, without any concern about whether anyone would think I was crazy. The sound was so alien and lonely, and filled with so much anguish, that I felt separate from it. Frightened by it.

I don't know how long I cried; I do know that eventually a cold wet nose pushed through my hands and Powder began licking the tears from my face.

I scooped him up and sat on my rear, next to Angie's grave, and rocked him back and forth as if he were a baby.

Eventually, he went to sleep.

I stood up, and Powder stirred, but he only nestled down further into my arms. I looked at him more closely. His coat was matted and filthy, and he had a nasty cut above his right eye. I would need to take him to the vet and get that looked at.

I looked down at Angie's grave. When I drove here, I thought I had so much to say. Now, I was at a loss for words.

I sighed.

"It's done," I said.

Then Powder and I got in the car and drove away.

"Oh, my dear Lord!"

Mrs. Hudson came running down the steps and yanked Powder from my arms.

"My poor little baby," she said, cuddling him to her. He looked up at her adoringly, as if he were really keen on the idea of being her poor little baby. No doubt he thought there might be dog biscuits involved.

Mrs. Hudson looked at me.

"You look a fright, Quinn," she said. "Why don't you go clean yourself up while I give Powder a bath."

"I think he might need to go to the vet," I said, pointing to the cut above his eye. It was crusted with blackened blood.

"Yes, yes, of course he does, after I clean him up. You go get yourself washed and you can drive us," she said, and the front door banged shut behind her.

I shrugged, and went upstairs to carry out my orders.

Chapter 36

Ramsey sat across from me at Scarlatti's Higher Grounds. Scarlatti's was my favorite new coffee place. I had chosen it because I knew Ramsey would be slightly uncomfortable here. Shame on me.

"You're telling me you haven't slept in a year," he said.

"That's right." I sipped my mocha and watched his face. "Not one single minute."

"And you expect me to believe that."

"Yep."

He swirled his coffee with a spoon and watched as Tina, the newest of Scarlatti's waitresses, skittered by in her official uniform. Who knew that a burgundy golf shirt and white shorts could look so good?

"That is medically impossible," Ramsey said at last. "To not sleep for a year."

"Yeah, that's what my doctor thought too. But here I am, sleepless in Spokane."

If he got the joke, he didn't give any sign. My guess was he hadn't seen many Nora Ephron movies.

"And you can function normally?" he said.

"More or less," I said. "It was rough for a while, but since the Idaho thing, I haven't had any blackouts. So it would seem I've adapted."

He drank some coffee and stared out the window. The sun was bright, and Riverfront Park was filled with people out enjoying the day.

I watched a teenager throwing Frisbee with his dog. It made me think of Powder. Mrs. Hudson would be taking him to Auntie Carla's Grooming today. When I got home the poor little guy would most likely have a blue ribbon in his hair. I would have to wait until Mrs. Hudson went to sleep to take the ribbon out.

"So, have you decided what you're going to do now?" he asked.

I watched his face. I still hadn't figured out whether Ramsey had befriended me because he liked me, or because he was still trying to figure out what had really happened that night in Idaho. He never said so, but I'm sure he didn't think self-defense was the right answer. The question was, would it make a difference if he knew the truth?

"Well, I've put most of the insurance money into an annuity," I said. "So I guess I don't have to work for a living."

He didn't say anything, just sipped his coffee.

"I've decided that I want to help people."

He set the coffee cup down.

"You're giving some of the money to charity?" he said. He sounded slightly surprised.

"Not exactly," I said. "I'm starting up my own little business. Helping people."

His eyebrows moved closer together.

"Helping them do what?" he asked.

"Find answers," I said. "Seek justice."

I flipped a business card across the table to him. He picked it up, read it, and stared at me.

"You're kidding," he said.

I shook my head.

"You need a license to do this kind of work."

"I have one," I said. "Want to see it?"

"No."

He laid the card on the table.

"Quinn, don't you think—"

"Save it, Ramsey," I said. He shrugged, threw a five on the table, and stood up.

"Okay," he said. "But try to stay out of trouble."

He shook his head.

"Just what I need," he said. "An amateur making my life miserable. Just don't start thinking my name is Lestrade and yours is Holmes, OK?"

I was shocked. A Sherlock Holmes reference. From Stan Ramsey.

"Stan, this couldn't mean you've actually read a book, could it?"

He turned and left. He was given to melodrama like that, but I liked him anyway.

I picked up my new business card and looked at it.

"Quinn Black Investigations. Justice Never Sleeps"

I tucked the card back into my pocket, and looked out the window at the park.

It was a nice day. The blues were blue, and the greens were green.

I might be a killer, but I wasn't a murderer. I felt pretty sure of that.

I smiled, and waited for Tina to refill my coffee.